The Struggles of Trying to be Mexican American Enough

Jonatán Noriega

Thank you to everybody who shared their stories so others could relate.

Editing Credits: Alan Alberto Corrales, Victoria Robertson, and Jennifer Muñoz.

Any events or characters depicted in the story are fictional. Similarities to any person, place, or idea are coincidental and not intended.

Table of Content

Table of Content

To find your identity is your one true purpose on this earth.

-Unknown

Los Fireworks

"There was a small crack in the window, and with help from the dust floating in the room, I could see a ray of light coming in. I could hear a light breeze outside, and it smelled like it was about to rain.

I had been tempted to look out the window. I just wanted to be out there. So, I kept trying to peek, hoping to see something. Even though we had been here for hours, everything was still unfamiliar.

It was dark outside when we arrived here. I didn't know where I was. I didn't recognize anything. I felt lost.

"Aléjate de la ventana,"[1] I heard a man yell.

I looked at my brother as he shoved away from the window. I didn't appreciate getting yelled at, but my brother shoving me was agitating.

I wondered how much longer we'd have to be in this room.

"¿Cuánto más tenemos que estar aqui?"[2] I asked him.

"No sé," he said.

I hated being inside, especially in this cold, sad room.

I closed my eyes and tried to imagine myself back home, but reality hit me.

I heard a knock at the door as more people were arriving. The room slowly filled up with strangers.

None of us had showered in days, but it wasn't the smell that bothered me, but just the number of strangers in the room. Who were they? Where did they come from?

I noticed a man with a gun on his waist walking in behind them.

---

[1] Get away from the window.
[2] How much longer do we have to be here?

1

The silent room got quieter, and everybody looked at him when he walked in.

When he entered, he grabbed my brother, Christian, and directed him into a separate room. He was in there for a while. I didn't know what was happening; I just knew I had to wait. He was in there for a few minutes, but it was long enough to make me anxious.

Finally, Christian came outside. He didn't say anything, but he looked concerned, which made me worry.

He sensed that I was disturbed but assured me everything was okay.

It was getting late, so he told me to go to sleep and that he would watch over my sister and me while we slept, but I didn't want to sleep. I was fully awake, but I drifted off after a couple of hours of sitting there quietly.

In the middle of the night, I suddenly woke up; I was disoriented and couldn't see anything.

"Levántate, vámonos,"[3] Christian whispered as he shook me.

"¿Para dónde vamos?"[4]

"Shhh… No hagas ruido"[5], he said.

I looked at him as he held my sister and walked towards the door. He made sure not to make any noise as they snuck out.

I tried to follow them, but I accidentally tripped and fell to the floor since I was half asleep. When I looked up, I made eye contact with a young woman sitting there.

I'll never forget her face; she was awake. She had been awake for a while and saw everything happening, but she didn't say anything, and I am thankful for that.

At the time, I had no idea why we had left, and once we were outside, Christian uttered, "Tenemos dos opciones,

---

[3] Get up and let's go.
[4] Where are we going?
[5] Don't make any noise.

podemos encontrar a alguien que nos lleve al otro lado, o nos podemos regresar a casa, pa' Cuernavaca."[6]

"¿Qué vamos a hacer?"[7] I asked him.

"No sé,"[8] he said as he was rummaging through our bags, trying to find a piece of paper with phone numbers written on it.

While he was doing that, I wondered if going back home was a better option, but we started walking before I could say anything.

We walked towards the city as the sun was rising behind the clouds.

Once we arrived, Christian told us to wait on the side of the road. There was a bench in the shade, but it was made out of metal, and the paint was peeling. It wasn't very comfortable.

"Cuídala,"[9] he said as he left.

We didn't have anything to entertain ourselves with. Plus, we were hungry and didn't have the energy to do much. I thought about going to a nearby store but was nervous about leaving and wary of strangers.

After a couple of hours, Christian returned with a man. The sun was now directly above us. It was hotter than before, and I was hungrier than ever.

"Él nos va a cruzar,"[10] he said.

I figured we weren't going home.

He grabbed my backpack and took out all the money we had stashed inside a pair of socks. Every single cent we had, I hoped this worked because we didn't have any more money for food, water, or to get back home.

---

[6] We have two options, we can find somebody else to take us, or we can go back home.

[7] What are we going to do?

[8] I don't know.

[9] Take care of her.

[10] He's going to help us cross.

I was tired and afraid of going into another safe house. I didn't want to be locked up in a room again.

However, this time it was different. We arrived at a house where people were waiting outside under a tree.

As soon as we sat down, I saw people forming a line at a water faucet.

People filled gallons with water, and we were advised to do the same. It was going to be a long trip.

After I filled my gallon, I took a small sip but was interrupted because we had to leave shortly.

The sun was hidden behind the clouds, but it was already setting.

We picked up our water jugs and began to walk. They were heavy but valuable, especially in our journey through the desert.

We walked for an hour before I saw the border.

I had never seen such a lengthy wall before. I could tell there was barbed wire; it all looked dangerous. My arms were starting to get sore and fatigued from carrying my own gallons of water. Christian noticed but couldn't help me since he was already carrying my sister's water; her arms had already given out.

The closer we got, the taller the walls grew, so I wondered, *how are we supposed to climb over it.*

A couple of drops of water hit the top of my head, so I looked up at the gray sky. It was lovely, and I was hoping for more, but it was a short feeling. It was just a light sprinkle, and after a few minutes, the water was gone. No puddles; it was like it had not rained at all.

The wall was about a kilometer away.

"No tenemos que brincar para cruzar," he explained, "Si se fijan bien hay un hueco por donde podemos—"[11]

He was interrupted by a loud noise.

PIF. PAH. BANG. BANG.

---

[11] We don't have to jump to cross it, if you look closely you can see that.

It was too dark for me to see what was going on. I just saw small blazes of light speeding past me. Christian threw the water gallons and picked up my sister as he ran towards the wall.

"No te fijes, córrele,"[12] he yelled at me.

I was overcome by confusion and adrenaline. I tried holding on tightly but decided to drop the water and run. Hoping not to trip, Christian looked at me and reminded me not to look back. I just kept seeing my shadow in front of me.

I had never seen fireworks like this before."

---

[12] Don't look back, just run.

El Pan Dulce

"I realized everybody had run, leaving me behind. I was scared and alone." He continued.

"*Me dejaron.*[13] I thought to myself, but it wasn't their fault. This was about survival.

I wanted to run, but I was too tired. I couldn't concentrate on what I was doing. That's when I felt liquid running down my leg. I was afraid it was blood. The adrenaline must have numbed me from feeling any pain.

I realized that it wasn't blood.

I wet myself out of fear.

I had not peed myself since that one winter night years ago when Christian hogged the whole blanket and left me on the cold floor.

I just kept moving, trying not to fall.

It took me a while to find the gap. Once over, I still had to keep going. The noises had stopped, but bright red and blue lights began flashing. I hid until the lights disappeared.

I didn't know where anybody was, so I ran for a few minutes. Until I saw a group of people congregating. I saw my sister sitting by herself and Christian talking to the adults. They were scolding him. Yelling at him for bringing us along and putting us in danger.

I tried to speak up, but I couldn't say anything. Everything began to slow down, and it got quieter. I began to feel dizzy and nauseous.

I didn't feel well.

Christian noticed me stumbling and tried to grab me, but he was too slow.

I collapsed on the ground.

---

[13] They abandoned me.

When I was on the floor, Christian touched my head. It was hot, my mouth was dry, and so was my tongue.

"Esta deshidratado,"[14] somebody said, and they handed my brother a bottle to give me.

He said he had to open the bottle before he gave it to me, but I looked at him and told him I had an accident.

He looked at me and told me not to worry, but I was uncomfortable. I wanted to change, so I got up and went behind a tree that shielded me from everybody.

I didn't know what to do with the dirty clothes, so I just threw them away. It wasn't environmentally friendly.

When I returned, I saw Christian had opened the bottle, so he handed it to me.

Out of everything it could have been, it was beer.

Warm, bitter, disgusting beer. I didn't know what was making me sicker, dehydration or the beer, but I didn't have many options, so I drank it.

I wanted to rest, but we had to keep going unless we wanted to be left behind. We walked as I sipped my Tecate.

We continued walking until the sun started rising again, and we reached a checkpoint. It didn't look like a safe house. It was much nicer and smelled better too.

Then some grandma came out and handed us a glass of milk and pan dulce.

Let me tell you, the pan was soft and warm, they weren't the most delicious conchas. They certainly had better pan dulce at the panadería[15] in my old neighborhood. But for some reason these were the best I had ever had.

Memories of my old home, neighborhood, and friends started to fill my head, and I started to feel sad, then I started getting tears in my eyes.

Christian saw me and told me that our ride was here. I knew he had caught me crying. I didn't like that. So, I wiped the tears off my face and followed him.

---

[14] He's dehydrated.
[15] Bakery

7

We saw a windowless van approaching. We got in, and all three of us sat in the back; I remember sitting there before falling asleep.

And that's how I started my new life in the States." said Frijolito.

El Paletero

When Frijolito[16] finished telling me his story, we were both quiet for a while. I didn't know what to say or do. I had questions, but I didn't know how to ask them.

I built up the courage to ask him where his parents were. He told me they were already here in the United States. They had traveled months prior, and once they had a home his parents sent for them.

I couldn't imagine traveling alone or my mom making me go by myself. She always goes with me to the store, to school, and even when I go to the ice cream truck.

I think that has to do with the fact that when I was younger, I went through my mother's purse to buy ice cream. I didn't understand the concept of money, so I just took a bill and ran outside when I heard the familiar jingle.

I didn't know what I could afford, so I just put the crisp bill on the counter. I asked what I could get, and he told me I could get a pack of candy cigarettes, an ice pop, a bag of chips, and a soda.

I had never gotten so much from the paletero[17] before; I felt so wealthy and satisfied.

That was until my mom saw me eating snacks on the front porch. She asked me where I got the money, and I told her it came from her purse. She went inside to check her purse, so I followed her but didn't understand the issue. I could tell she was upset, even mad, but she didn't hit me or yell. She just told me to go outside.

I walked out, and she came out with a small Big Bird yellow plastic chair. She told me to have a seat and wait for the paletero. I did just that. I sat outside for hours. Until the

---

[16] Small bean.
[17] The Ice Cream Man.

9

sun went down and all the street lights came on. My mom came out and told me to go inside and shower. The next day after school, she made me sit out there once again. I kept waiting for this man to come into our apartment complex. I just sat there waiting for the sound that had once brought me joy.

Day after day, I waited. Almost a whole week passed until I heard the little jingle. I ran inside and told my mom; she just told me to stay inside and ran off. I wanted to go outside with her, but I decided it was best to stay inside. I did run to the side window so I could at least see what was happening.

I just remember seeing my mom climb into the ice cream truck and running out with a couple of ice pops and a fistful of random candies. I heard her running down the hallway and slam the door shut.

I looked at her, stunned, while she caught her breath. Then she just said, "No me quiso dar la feria…"[18] as she winked at me and handed me an ice pop. She was determined to get her money back, one way or another.

I paused and realized that my story was nothing like his. My story was not about a dangerous passage. He risked his life to reach the States while I was born here. I didn't have to go through that and thought, *Damn, I'm Mexican, but I'm not that Mexican.*

I looked over at him, and he just smiled at me.

"Ya duérmete, Xavi,"[19] he said.

"Goodnight, Frijolito," I responded softly, as I laid there thinking about what I had just learned.

---

[18] He didn't want to give me the change.
[19] Go to sleep Xavi.

Mexican American Autobiography

My name is Xavier Barrera, which differs in
pronunciation depending on who says it. The most common
way it's pronounced is "Ha-Vi-Er." Most Mexicans or people
who speak Spanish pronounce it this way. Then there are
those who don't speak Spanish or prefer to call me "Ex-Ay-
Vi-Er." I grew up speaking Spanish, so I just went by "Ha-
Vi." My mom would even call me that unless I was in
trouble. Then she would yell my full name, it wasn't very
long, but I knew the difference.

I quickly realized that people had multiple names. Two
first and two last names. Like, who has two names? Also,
what is the purpose of having two last names? I didn't
understand that concept, I think one name is OK, but I
believe that since I only have one first name. When I asked
my mom why I only had one name, she said it was because,
initially, the doctors told her she was having a daughter. She
spent months planning and coming up with the perfect name.
"Melissa Nicole Barrera." Melissa because during the spring,
she would see all the bees flying around the flowers working
hard to make honey. She loved that time of year and just
being surrounded by nature. Since it was her favorite treat
and "Melissa" means "honeybee," it seemed like a perfect
fit. Nicole came from a childhood friend she had not seen in
years but constantly thought about.

Turned out I was, in fact, not a daughter but rather a son,
so she just named me Xavier. I was pretty disappointed when
I asked her why she chose that name, and she told me that it
was the first name on the last page of the name catalog. I felt
like there was no deeper meaning to my name. It felt like

there was no history, no sense of identity, just a simple name.

I also only have one last name, my mom's, not my father's. I don't know if he died, got deported, was imprisoned, or just didn't want to be here. I'm okay with this. At least, that's what I keep telling myself.

I grew up in Phoenix, Arizona. The city is known for being too hot and is a perfect grid. I eventually got used to the heat, but it never allowed me to play outside over the summer. Unless I played in the middle of the night, and even then, I could still feel it.

I didn't always have friends, so playing sports was all I had. I had always preferred soccer over basketball and football. I don't know many Mexicans that play in the NBA or NFL, but I know a bunch of Mexicans that play soccer.

I was okay with my mediocre playing skills since my mom never pressured me into sports. She always kept up with all my games. She wouldn't always go due to work but would ask me, "If I had fun." She supported me, which was the best. Plus, I just liked playing. It brought me a sense of joy.

Even though I played sports, I'm overly sensitive too. I mean, I don't fit the "Machista"[20] molds. I have always been embarrassed about my sensitivity. I grew up thinking that it was a flaw. But, like my name, it is a part of my identity.

Another part of who I am is the fact that I have ADHD. Something that would be undiagnosed for most of my childhood. I guess mental illnesses are more like myths in many Mexican households, like the chupacabras, but not like the "La Llorona"; she's real, according to my mom.

So, it was just me and my mom, who would hit me with the occasional "Te calmas o te calmo"[21] when I was misbehaving.

---

[20] A man who believes that women are inferior to men.
[21] A Mexican saying that promotes good behavior. "Calm down, or I'll calm you down."

But she was also the same mom who worked for the same pharmaceutical company in the sanitation department her entire adult life. Her job was to make sure that the labs were sanitized and germ-free. In the beginning, she worked way over 40 hours a week. She was the only one who sanitized it since it was a small laboratory. Still, as it expanded, she got promoted and eventually became the director of the sanitation administration. Only she had to enroll in night classes so she could learn English. The company appreciated her hard work and dedication and even helped her get her residency. Then she began to work fewer hours.

All that hard work meant she had to sacrifice some things. She wasn't around when I was a toddler. There are a ton of baby pictures in an old photo album of me living in Mexico without my mom, mostly of me eating dirt. Still, I don't remember that part of my life. My mom sent me to live with my grandma for a couple of years, she lost those years so I could be taken care of, and when she had a stable lifestyle, I moved back. Luckily it was right before the start of school.

My grandma said she took me to the border and gave me to another old lady. Since my grandma couldn't cross, the lady was my mule. This was when grandparents could cross their grandchildren, and no questions were asked.

Besides living in Mexico for a couple of years, my childhood was pretty ordinary. The last summer before my first day of school, I had friends I would play with daily.

I don't remember their names, but we would ride our bikes unless yours was stolen, then you had to ride on the back of somebody's bike on top of the pegs. Or as we called them, "Diablitos," which translated to little devils.

I never understood why. But there were many things about the language I didn't understand. Like why did we say "Dieciocho" to mean "Tag" when it means eighteen, or why we would shout out "Klin" to mean timeout.

This meant that my difficulties with language were magnified, and that the beauty of language was lost.

I didn't understand that language didn't have to translate for people to understand what was being said.

Noriega

Morehouse Elementary

I remember being excited about school at some point in my life. At least, I think I was enthusiastic, it all feels like a distant memory, but I'm pretty sure something happened that changed that. I don't know if everybody experiences school the same way. You start with dreams, and then school begins to slowly kill them. Maybe that is the whole purpose of school; to slowly squeeze any hopes and dreams you may have until you no longer like school. Then blame you for being a failure.

I like the idea of school, don't get me wrong. Learning new information is great, but at some point, school becomes a nightmare.

My first day of school was a cultural shock. My mom didn't get a spot for me at my neighborhood school since I had enrolled so late, so I had to go to the one a couple of blocks away. Kids kept asking me my name, and I didn't understand what was happening. I had never heard English before.

I told my mom that people kept talking to me, but none of it made sense. She tried convincing me that I would make friends, now let me tell you, she was wrong about that.

Now being a minority is one thing, but being a minority amongst minorities is a concept that is difficult to understand and impossible to explain. I knew there were other Mexicans in the world, so I never thought I would be the only one.

I was the only Mexican student in an all-Black elementary.

Growing up in Morehouse Elementary, I felt different. It had nothing to do with race. It was something deeper than that.

From the first day of school, I had to leave everything that reminded me of who I was at home. I couldn't carry any

15

of it. I tried speaking Spanish to my classmates, but none of them understood what I was saying.

I did try to convince some of my classmates to learn Spanish.

That was until Ms. Skains scolded me.

"We don't speak Spanish here," she yelled as she threw a book at me. Which is illegal, but I didn't know this at the time.

This happened in front of all the students. A classmate was trying to learn different words in Spanish. He would try his best to repeat whatever I had just said and laugh. I enjoyed being his teacher. I was about to translate. "Pendejo"[22] when I heard her voice. Probably wasn't the most appropriate vocabulary to teach, but she didn't know the language.

Her voice was frightening and authoritative. I froze up; I didn't know what to say to the rest of my classmates. I just stared at them, and they just looked back at me. I felt embarrassed, awkward, and ashamed.

Above all, I felt small, tiny, but somehow, I   wanted to shrink in my seat and disappear. I guess I was too Mexican to fit in.

After that, I was always afraid to speak Spanish in school.

I was also reluctant to speak English because I knew so little. Spelling test would be returned stained with red ink. Not my fault that words in English aren't spelled how they sound. What kind of language does that? Any English I did know came from cartoons, but those words weren't part of our weekly vocabulary.

I learned how to say simple words, mostly cuss words.

Because became "be-ka- ü-se", Wednesday became "Wed-nes-day" and comfortable became "Com-for-table"

Every language learner's essential vocabulary, but that is pretty much all I had.

---

[22] Stupid

After a while, I figured out what made me different from my peers.

It was the language barrier that made me feel alone. My teachers were either Black or Euro-American. My teachers might have had their differences, but at least they all had the same language. I didn't have a Mexican teacher, and I certainly didn't have a teacher that understood my struggles with language. I was all alone in this world.

Los Conquistadores

During my first Social Studies class, we learned about the history of the United States.

"In 1492, Christopher Columbus discovered America," said Mr. Thomas, "And thanks to his discovery, Indians and Black people were able to flourish here."

I sat there thinking about what he said. I wondered what he meant by discovered. *How was it possible to discover a land where people were already living?*

"Mr. Columbus was trying to find a route to India but stumbled across something much better."

I remember sitting in class when Mr. Thomas turned towards me and said, "Thanks to him, people like you can practice your language. He saved you. If it weren't for him you would still be praying to your sun and water god."

I didn't understand what he meant, but I wanted to learn about my old gods, and it also seemed like Christopher Columbus was a nice person for doing that.

"The Spanish were conquistadors," he exclaimed as he showed us images of men in suits of armor.

"Hernan Cortez, Francisco Pizarro, Miguel Holguin..." he said as he switched slides.

"They conquered the Americas, giving the savages trade, developed new technologies, religion, and slavery."

"Isn't slavery bad," interrupted Lyric, one of my classmates.

"No," he responded.

I looked at her confused because I had never heard of people owning people before.

Lyric snapped back and mentioned how conquistadors destroyed families and enslaved innocent people.

Noriega

However, Mr. Thomas explained, "Conquistadors traded with African countries and built relationships that helped develop their countries."

"Actually, during the Triangular Atlantic Slave trade, European countries started to trade guns and rum for slaves. The Europeans started an arms war since slavery became such a lucrative business. Therefore, kingdoms needed to protect themselves from slave raids. This caused wars to break out and had empires destroy themselves once weakened."

Lyric paused for a second, "Which made it easier to be conquered..." she said with anger in her eyes.

"Conquerors saved the savages.", was all Mr. Thomas said.

I loved that about her and was excited about the possibility of learning about my history, but that wouldn't be until later in life.

As for now, I continued to learn a history, that wasn't mine or from a perspective I was familiar with.

Everybody Speaks Spanish Here

I always loved going to the store with my mom. I had an irrational fear of being left alone at home. I was mostly afraid she wouldn't come back. I never told her that.

We didn't have a car, so we relied on public transportation. We caught the bus a block around the house, and after a couple of stops, we would be at our destination.

This store was special because once inside, mostly everybody spoke Spanish. Even the music inside the stores would be in Spanish. I always wanted to have the job of getting to pick what song would be next.

I loved going in. There were so many smells. We would always go to the fruit and vegetable section first. We would grab some apples, oranges, and bananas, and sometimes we would get watermelon if they were in season. We never got any fancy fruits like kiwis, strawberries, or any of the berries, for that matter. They were too expensive for us.

As long as I got to slap my rice bag or put my hands in the open bean container. I was one happy child.

"Saca las manos de los frijoles,"[23] my mom would yell.

I knew putting my hands inside the bean container was wrong, even unsanitary, but it was satisfying.

At the end of every shopping spree, my mom would let me have one snack from the store. I wasn't interested in any candy, chips, or pan dulce.[24] I could get those anywhere.

No, what I wanted was an aguas fresca.

There were so many flavors. I think my favorite was limonada. After that, it was a tie between agua de melon and

---

[23] Get your hands out of the bean container.
[24] Sweet bread

agua de coco. Depending on who had made them. That was my favorite part, except for the time that I dropped my cup. It wasn't my fault, you see.

So, what happened was I had just gotten my limonada, and I was making my way back to my mother. When I turned the corner, I saw two Black men talking. I was shocked, speechless, and flabbergasted. I learned that word in school; it means surprised or something like that.

I dropped my cup and ran to get my mom.

When I found her, she followed me to where I dropped my cup. When we arrived, she saw my cup on the floor and told me she was not getting me another one. I gave her a side-eye and pointed to what I had just discovered.

"Ama, están hablando en español," I told her, "Y son negros."[25]

I was astonished.

Stunned.

Fascinated.

My notion of who spoke Spanish and who didn't was turned upside down.

Maybe Mexicans had taught them Spanish in school, I thought.

My mom, on the other hand, was not impressed. She was more embarrassed than anything else.

The men introduced themselves politely and fist-bumped me. It was the greatest moment of my life. Then they said they were from "La Dominica,"[26,] and they laughed.

I didn't know where that was or if they were laughing at me or with me. But I didn't care.

As my mom dragged me through the store, I couldn't help but smile. I had seen something I had never experienced before. It was like seeing a unicorn in the wild.

They speak Spanish, I thought to myself.

I suddenly didn't feel so alone.

---

[25] Mom, they're speaking Spanish, and they're black.
[26] Dominican Republic

However, as soon as I got to school, I knew none of this would matter.

El Tlaloc [27]

My life remained constant for a couple of years. Nothing new, or anything I remember, until I was in middle school. That year I wasn't a loner at school. I did eventually make one friend. Well, he was more of an acquaintance. But after years of being alone in school, it felt great to not be by myself.

His name was Kevin Robinson. We only met because our 7th-grade English teacher, Ms. Neal, put us together as reading partners. Turned out his English was just as bad as mine.

Kevin was tall, muscular, and athletic, especially for a middle school student. He would always push me to play basketball during lunch. Kevin would never play soccer whenever I asked him to. He would always complain that it would "mess up his kicks". Teachers considered him a bad kid because he was too talkative and had no self-control. The truth was that I didn't have any self-control either. I just didn't feel comfortable talking, so I got labeled as "developing".

We did have some similarities; we both needed to get out of our seats and walk around. Sometimes we would even be in detention during lunch together. Which was often. We spent most of the year eating inside the ISS room. We had matching black Jansport backpacks, so there was enough for us to be friends.

Whenever Ms. Neal would ask me a question, he would blurt out, "No comprende,"[28,] and the whole class would laugh at me.

---

[27] Aztec God of rain
[28] He does not understand.

I hated that I didn't fully understand what was going on, but I understood enough to know what was happening. I hated not being able to defend myself. I hated not being able to piece words together to form a sentence that would describe how I was accurately feeling. I hated that language was still a barrier for me.

He would always call me names, especially when we were around girls.

However, he was the only kid that would talk to me.

He would never bully me when it was just us two and always said, "X, you know I'm just messing with you." I guess that was his way of apologizing when he realized I was hurt. The truth is that it wasn't his jokes that hurt; it was the reality that I was labeled as a slow learner. It wasn't my fault I was raised with a different language. I could still learn, but not everybody saw that in me.

Despite all the hardships, we realized that we were all we had at school.

Kevin lived in the same apartment complex as me. We would never sit together on our way to school, but on the way home, we sometimes sat together in the back.

Our teachers weren't right about much, sometimes, I wondered how they were qualified to teach, but they were right about one thing. Man could Kevin talk. He would talk the whole ride home. Most of the time, Kevin would talk about girls, who he liked that day, or was obsessing about. If not that, then sports or what teacher he hated. I would just listen and agree with him, except for one time.

However, that day the ride had been unusually quiet. He didn't say anything. Then he broke the silence and said, "I feel different."

It felt like a random comment; there was no context. Nothing to help me understand what he was talking about. There were no context clues or anything else teachers would tell us to look for to understand what was happening.

"I feel like I'm misunderstood," he continued.

I didn't completely understand what he was saying, but for some unfamiliar reason, I could relate to him. I nodded. This was the first time I had agreed with him. It made me realize even though he was a dick to me, he was the closest person I had to a friend.

When we hopped off the bus in front of our complex, he asked me if I was doing anything later, which was the first time he asked me to hang out outside of school.

Since nobody was home, I suggested we go watch some cartoons. He looked at me and smiled. I had a key to my apartment, so I unlocked the door, and we walked in.

I noticed a stack of bills, some letters, and an envelope with the words "Renta"[29] on the kitchen counter.

I looked through the envelopes, not because I was nosy. My mom would just make me read and translate whatever was being said. Whenever I didn't understand something, she would be amazed that my middle school English was not preparing me to be able to comprehend house loan contracts, eviction notices, or paperwork that had to do with immigration status.

She would ask, "¿Entonces que estas aprendiendo?"[30]

Well, Mom, I learned about SOH CAH TOA today and that mitochondria are the powerhouse of a cell.

I went to turn on the T.V., but Kevin had other plans. He asked me if I wanted to make it rain.

"Make it rain?" I said, slightly confused.

"Yeah, wey," he said. I had just taught him that word.

He went up to the side window and started throwing envelopes. I just saw them glide through the air. It was peaceful.

We threw one envelope at a time until there was only one left. I grabbed the envelope that read "Renta" and threw it over too.

---

[29] Rent
[30] Then what are you learning?

As soon as it left my hand, I made eye contact with my mom, who had just parked and was underneath us, watching this all unfold.

"Xavier Barrera!" she yelled at me.

But it was too late. I had already thrown the envelope over the ledge and to make matters worse, the envelope was not sealed shut. I just stood there as the money slipped out and fluttered like hummingbirds flying from flower to flower.

I could just see the terror in my mother's eyes. I'm pretty sure she saw the fear in my eyes too. I can't remember the date, but it was definitely going on my tombstone.

I couldn't do anything but watch my mom pick up pieces of cash and envelopes scattered all over the parking lot. I looked over at Kevin, but he was already gone. I'm telling you, he was an intelligent kid. He knew when to bounce.

I didn't know what to do. I just waited in there. I wondered if I should go find a belt myself and be proactive or just be patient. Either way, I knew what was coming.

I had never gotten whooped like that before. I guess that was the day I learned to have common sense.

If you're wondering if it hurt, "Yeah, me dolió."[31]

We had to move after that.

My mom told me we were moving because we were being evicted. She convinced me that she was not able to recover some of the bills. As we were packing, I felt guilty. I thought it was my fault, but it turns out she had gotten approved for a house loan. She hit me with that Mexican guilt trip.

I was sad. But I didn't cry. I didn't have much holding me here. I was okay with the change. That was until she told me we were moving into a Mexican community. That's when I really got scared.

---

[31] It hurt.

Chaparral Middle School

I didn't get to finish 7th grade at Morehouse or say bye to Kevin. I simply disappeared, like a ghost. It all happened so fast; one moment, I was in an apartment complex, and after just one day of packing, we were gone.

It was an empty experience, it wasn't the prettiest place in the world, but it was my home. All I could do was look forward to my new life.

Before unpacking our moving boxes, my mom drove me to the neighborhood school, Chaparral Middle School. She told me I could go in or wait in the car. I stayed in the car. I knew I had to be a new student once again. I wanted to be excited, but something was holding me back.

On the drive to our new house, I looked out the window and saw a park nearby, there was also a carnicería,[32] a panadería, and it was closer to the store with the aguas frescas. I loved my new neighborhood.

There was a lot of art here too. Not just graffiti but large murals, some filled with roses, one that included a skull. There were lots of them in different designs and styles. There was one of a man in front of a field, with the name "Cesar," and a quote underneath that read, "Sí Se Puede"[33]. I wondered who he was or what he had done.

I loved my new home too. It was a small house, but it had two rooms. Which was more than we needed. It wasn't in perfect condition, but it was better than the apartment we spent years at.

My mom also informed me that there would be some changes this year. Instead of relying on the school bus, I

---

[32] Butcher shop
[33] Yes, it is possible.

would have to walk. It was only a few blocks away, and I was old enough to walk alone.

On my first day of school, I walked by myself since my mom had to work in the morning. I was running a little late, so I went in as the bell rang. I overheard kids speaking in Spanish.

Speaking Spanish in school? I thought puzzled.

I wanted to fit in, but I realized their Spanish was almost perfect. Where my Spanish was a combination of "Spanglish" and "Mocho"[34], I wasn't comfortable. I wanted to avoid any conversation in English and Spanish.

I looked down at my schedule and tried to find my classroom. I felt some kid bump into me, which made me drop my paper schedule.

He must not have seen me, I thought.

Then I saw him turn towards me. It looked like he was about to apologize and pick up my schedule. Instead, he kicked it as he walked away laughing.

I started feeling insecure, but then I heard the late bell. I wasn't lost. I just didn't know where to go. I began to feel overwhelmed, like I was about to cry, but luckily a hall monitor saw me and tried to help me. I told her I had lost my schedule, and she told me we would get another one.

After I got my new schedule, she walked me to class. I went inside and looked around; I didn't know anybody. I wondered who all these new kids were, but I was the new kid. I had never been in a classroom with so many Mexicans before. I walked in and saw an empty desk. I walked straight to it.

I didn't know what to say. Every single person in this room looked just like me. Well, except for the teacher. Ms. Boyd was a white lady in her late 30s. There wasn't anything special about her. She had red hair and had probably been teaching for a decade. She walked like she was always in a hurry.

---

[34] Somebody who speaks broken Spanish.

Noriega

Every morning, the whole class had breakfast in our homeroom. Muffins were on the menu today. Not my favorite, but it would get me to lunch. I was hungry, but I was shy. I knew I would regret it if I didn't get breakfast, but I was too scared to get one.

A kid sitting in front of me turned around to face me.

"Eyt ¿Cómo te llamas?"[35], he asked.

I just looked at him and said, "I don't speak Spanish."

He turned back around.

I sat there, "Why did I lie about that? I do know Spanish."

This doesn't make any sense. I noticed another kid laughing at me. I didn't understand whether he was laughing at me or the situation.

He looked at me and said, "Me llamo Luis Ernesto Flores Bravo, but people call me Frijolito."[36]

"Frijolito?" I asked, stunned.

"Like little bean," he added.

I realized I spoke Spanish and wondered, *How did he know I was lying.*

He put his hand out to greet me.

I just looked at him. I didn't know what to do.

The bell rang, and Ms. Boyd announced, "Time to go to your first period."

We all got up and left for our next classes. I didn't see Frijolito again that day, not in any of my classes, lunch, or recess. It was like I had made him up.

---

[35] What is your name?

[36] My name is Luis Ernesto Flores Bravo, but you can call me Frijolito.

Damaged Tongue

The following morning, I sat next to Frijolito during breakfast.

He asked me, "Why did you lie?"

I pretended like I didn't know what he was talking about. Instead of answering the question, I asked him where he had been all day.

He looked confused, "I went with Ms. Muñoz," he said.

"Who is Ms. Muñoz?" I asked.

"Ms. Muñoz is the ELD teacher."

"ELD?" I responded.

Frijolito explained that it was a class for kids who were behind academically in English, either because they had low test scores or didn't know English in general.

I asked, "Is everybody in that class Mexican?"

"No, Hasan is in that class," he said as he pointed to a Middle Eastern kid in our classroom.

"Tambien Gitego, and Jiste" he continued "But, no están aquí."[37]

"How do you get out," I asked.

"You have to test out," he explained.

"Test out to be in regular classes?" I was confused.

"Yeah, you know how you have English, Social Studies, and Science. Well, we just have ELD all day."

"Do you like it?" I asked, curious to see how he felt about that class.

"For the most part, yeah, I'm a better reader than most of the other kids in my class, so I know nobody will make fun of me because we are all struggling."

There was a pause.

---

[37] Gitego and Jiste both have that class, but they're not here today.

Noriega

"I mean, one-time Ms. Muñoz made us sing in front of the school, which was pretty embarrassing."

"She made you sing in front of the whole school?"

"Yeah, it was stupid."

"How do you feel about missing out on classes?"

"I mean, I struggle in them, so I need the help. I even struggle in math."

"Yeah, those equations can get complex," I said.

"I don't struggle with the equations or the numbers," he said, "I don't understand what they are asking. Numbers are the same in any language." He added.

I had never thought of that before. I guess he was right about that.

"Plus, Ms. Muñoz lets us speak Spanish," he said as an added surprise.

"You can speak Spanish in that class?" I asked, surprised.

"Yeah."

"Why?"

"I don't know; she doesn't like to punish students for using Spanish. She says it's part of our identity and that if she took it away, we would eventually lose it and never pass it on to other generations. That taking language from people can be traumatic and stunt our growth. Algo así, la verdad no le entiendo."[38]

I didn't know who Ms. Muñoz was or what trauma meant, but I wanted to meet her.

The bell rang, and Frijolito asked me to walk him to class. We walked to the other side of campus. I knew I would be late, but I didn't mind.

We got to a door, and there was a sign that read, Ms. Muñoz. The door was decorated. It had a female face on it; I didn't know who she was. I saw a face with a unibrow on it, and her head was filled with flowers. I had never seen a decorated door before.

---

[38] Something like that, I don't really understand what she means.

I saw a teacher open the door to greet her students. She was beautiful; she had thick curly dark hair. Before I could get a real look, Frijolito interrupted me, "She's pretty, huh," he implied.

I turned and looked at him. Before I could say anything, he finished, "I'll show you her Instagram later. See you at lunch."

Los Nicknames

During lunch, we sat together. Frijolito talked to me about his class and what he had learned. I had never actually spoken about class with anybody before.

Before I said anything, he froze. He looked at me, and I saw he was thinking about something.

"¿Como te llamas?"[39]

It had occurred to me that I had not told him my name. I thought about it for a second. I knew my name, but how I pronounced it in Spanish or English would shape my identity at this new school.

Finally, I said, "My name is "Ha-Vi-Er," but you can call me "Ha-vi."

We shook hands; it felt formal. I couldn't help but laugh. I liked my new friend.

"Nice to meet you, Luis," I added.

"Frijolito," he corrected.

At recess, we both ran into the field. Frijolito passed me the ball and was surprised when I shot it, hitting the crossbar. He didn't expect me to be a soccer player. I told him I didn't play much but always enjoyed it.

Then the bell rang.

I asked him to help me find my next class since I had different electives that day.

I read, "Mrs. Clark, Music Room, G4."

He looked at me and said, "We have music together."

It was a pleasant surprise since I didn't like music class. Like most people, I like music, but producing enjoyable music is difficult. Plus, I had Mrs. Lamb for music class in first grade. She locked me in the closet because I was offbeat, but it wasn't my fault I didn't have rhythm.

---

[39] What's your name?

On our walk, Frijolito told me how much he loved that class. He didn't like Mrs. Clark, but he enjoyed the class. Frijolito shared how he used to play the drums, back home. Well, it wasn't an actual set of drums but rather a row of water buckets. All different sizes. He would take any branch he could find, and spend hours out there, banging away. Now that he was in the United States, he wanted to play a real instrument, like the bass or the piano.

That's when I realized that he was born in Mexico.

When we walked in, I saw Ms. Clark wouldn't be any different. I saw a picture of her on her desk. Her husband was a border patrol agent. I didn't want to assume she was racist, but her husband seemed to have rubbed off on her. I could tell she had prejudice towards certain students, especially Frijolito.

I felt like Ms. Clark's eyes were already on me.

"Hello, Mrs. Clark," said Frijolito.

She completely ignored him and snatched my schedule from my hands.

"Ex-Ay-Vi-Er," she said out loud.

"Ha-Vi," corrected Frijolito as we exchanged looks.

"That's not what it says here, Luis."

"Frijolito," I corrected as we both busted out laughing.

It turned out that Ms. Clark didn't appreciate the nicknames. We both got lunch detention for that. I was afraid my mom would find out, but she didn't.

I couldn't understand why I had received lunch detention, especially since there was no explanation. Every Mexican I knew had a nickname; my mom's name was "Guadalupe," which was shortened to "Lupita," and I have even heard people call her "Lupis." Her nickname had a nickname. I didn't understand why that had upset Ms. Clark. Maybe it was just a Mexican custom that she didn't understand.

The Pop Quiz

A week later, we were allowed back into class. However, not before we had an intervention.

There was a police officer on campus. I didn't know what he was there for, maybe to intimidate students. Before we were allowed back, we had a meeting with him. Officer Cox talked to us about being on our best behavior and not causing any trouble. Just us three in his office. I started feeling like I was in the middle of an interrogation. I didn't appreciate that.

As we sat there, I could tell that Frijolito was uncomfortable. He avoided making eye contact and kept touching his shoes.

Officer Cox noticed him starting to get fidgety and let us go. He handed us a pass that read, "Excuse the tardy."

It was a useless pass since we still had 5 minutes of recess left. Precisely enough time to do absolutely nothing. I told Frijolito that I was going to start walking to class.

He seemed distracted and in a hurry. Before he left, he asked me for the note, told me he would be a little late, and asked me to save him a seat. I didn't ask where he was going, but I just saw him walk towards the bathrooms, but those weren't even the nice bathrooms. If he was going to be late, I figured he was going to take a shit.

Why he didn't go to the nice bathroom in the back.

Before I could form a thought, I got distracted by the clouds. It was cloudy and smelled like rain.

I kept looking up at the sky as I walked to class, I heard the bell ring, so I went into class. Only a few students were sitting down.

As the late bell rang, Ms. Clark announced, "We have a pop quiz today."

Really, lady, a quiz in music class, I thought.

She explained that she would play songs and would have to identify them by name.

I knew I was going to fail before I even began the quiz.

She gave us a blank piece of paper.

"Now I will play you the songs in a random order, and you have to write down the name of them," she said.

She played,

> "Flight of the Bumblebee" by Rimsky-Korsakov,
> "Ode to Joy" by Beethoven,
> "Minute Waltz" by Chopin,
> "The Nutcracker" by Tchaikovsky,
> and
> "The Barber of Seville" by Gioachino Rossini.

Midway through the first song, Frijolito walked in; he seemed out of breath. *Must have been a tough shit*, I thought as I laughed to myself.

"Shh.", I heard as the music continued.

Annoyed that she had to stop playing, she took the note and read it. She handed him a quiz and kept her eyes on him until he sat beside me.

As he sat down, he winked at me. I couldn't control my laugh.

She continued playing.

She played the first song, and everybody started writing except me.

She did this for every song and then asked us to pass our quizzes forward. I was about to pass mine when Frijolito saw my page was blank. He quickly wrote answers down and handed them both in.

I was amazed.

How did he know? I wondered.

Then I figured he might have just written down random names. I mean, that was better than getting a zero.

Noriega

"Mi favorita es la de la bumblebee,"[40] he said as we left class, he also told me he would be late tomorrow. I then noticed that his knuckles were red. I asked him what happened. He just winked at me and left.

The following day, I didn't see him in homeroom. Which was expected. During lunch, I went to the snack bar and figured I'd buy him some chips or maybe a soda as a thank you. It had rained the night before, so we couldn't use the field.

I waited there for him on a bench but didn't see him. We didn't have music that day, so I wouldn't see him there either. He had disappeared once again.

After school, I started walking home when Frijolito walked up to me.

Surprised, I asked him where he had been all day.

"ISS."

"ISS? Why?" I asked, confused.

"Oh, Ms. Clark said I cheated on yesterday's quiz," he said nonchalantly.

"But you didn't cheat; I did," I said.

"Si, pero, you know my English isn't good, so she probably assumes I'm dumb, you know."

"But I'm the dumb one," I said.

"Yeah, I know," he responded.

I punched his shoulder as we both laughed.

I wanted to invite him over, so I did.

He agreed. I was excited, but I wanted to play it cool.

I was going to introduce my new friend to my mom.

---

[40] My favorite one is the bumblebee song.

Los Nopales

I noticed my mom's car was in the driveway, so I knew my mom was home. As excited as I was to introduce Frijolito to my mom, I was worried. I got flashbacks of the last time I brought a friend to my house. I didn't want to move again. I wondered if I was maybe making a mistake.

When I opened the door. I saw my mom in the kitchen making food.

"¿Quién es este fulano?"[41] she asked suspiciously as she tried to read him.

The room got tense, and I could see Frijolito getting uncomfortable.

"Su novio,"[42] said Frijolito.

"¿Tu novio?" she asked, perplexed.

"What the fu…." I began responding. As she gave me a look. I knew if I finished that sentence, it would be the last sentence I would say with a complete set of teeth.

"Buenas tardes suegra."[43]

"¿Suegra?" I said, looking back and forth during this conversation.

My mom couldn't contain her laugh.

Frijolito introduced himself, "Me llamo Luis Ernesto Flores Bravo. A sus órdenes."

"Gusto en conocerte," she replied, "¿De dónde eres?"[44]

Damn, mom, what's with the 50 questions? I thought.

"De Cuernavaca, Morelos," he responded, as I directed him into my room since the food was not ready yet.

---

[41] Who is this stranger?
[42] His boyfriend.
[43] Good afternoon mother-in-law.
[44] Where are you from?

We walked into my room, and Frijolito noticed my Hot Wheels collection.

"¿Por qué tienes tantos carritos?"[45]

"I've gotten them over the years. ¿Que tú no tienes?"[46]

He shook his head.

Maybe Mexicans don't believe their children should have childhoods, I thought.

I heard my mom yell out, "¿Listos para comer?"

I instantly became hungrier and began to wonder what she had made.

It smelled spicy. Maybe it was chile colorado,[47] or perhaps even birria. I was wrong. It was nopales[48], and I hate nopales. I didn't even know that they were. How could somebody eat something so green, slimy, sticky, and chewy? I mean, I had never eaten them, but that's what I imagined they would be like. Plus, I always found a way of getting out of it.

I saw a Maruchan cup with water on the counter. I let out a sigh of relief.

Frijolito, on the other hand, was surprisingly excited.

"Tengo días que se me han antojado nopales."[49]

I stared at Frijolito in disgust.

I looked at him, and while my mom got up, I said, "I know you're lying."

"What? I love nopales, you don't like them? They're a lot better than that Maruchan."

I shook my head, and we looked at each other as we ate.

"What kind of Mexican doesn't like nopales?" he asked.

I didn't respond, and I thought about it. I didn't know what kind of Mexican I was. I didn't know I had to like specific food.

---

[45] Why do you have so many toys?
[46] Don't you have any?
[47] Mexican beef stew
[48] Prickly Pear Cactus
[49] I have been craving nopales for days.

After a dinner filled with laughter and conversation, my mom offered him a ride home.

We got in our car, and we sat in the back. I was not used to sitting in the back since it was just my mom and me.

"Cinturones,"[50] said my mom as we clicked our seatbelts. When my mom turned on the car, the radio started playing. It was the station my mom liked listening to, "La Caliente 103.2". As soon as the song came on, my mom and Frijolito started singing. They both knew this song; I had heard it before, but I didn't know the words like they did. I just mumbled what I knew and tried to keep up. Once it was over, I felt out of place. I started to get jealous of Frijolito.

He gave my mom directions, and we turned into a trailer park after a while.

"Ahi en la troca blanca,"[51] he said as he pointed to a white truck.

When we approached it, I saw the truck had its hood open.

I noticed an older teenager holding a flashlight and an older shirtless man yelling at him about holding it correctly as they worked on the truck. He had grease and oil stains all over his arms.

"Buenas Noches," said Frijolito as he walked in towards them.

My mom introduced herself and waved.

"Saluda,"[52] she said to me as she turned and looked at me. I waved at them as we drove away.

"He's nice," said my mom.

"Yeah," I responded.

It wouldn't be long before Frijolito would start spending every weekend with me. He talked to my mom about his soccer team and asked her to let me join. It was the first time I played soccer outside of recess.

---

[50] Buckle up
[51] There, by the white truck.
[52] Introduce yourself.

Bedtime Stories

Every Saturday looked the same. Every morning my mom would make us pancakes as we got ready. Frijolito would bring his soccer uniform and an extra pair of clothes. It wouldn't take us very long to get ready. When I first joined the team, some of the kids tried to pick on me. I didn't know these kids. They went to different middle schools. They tried to kick my backpack around, but Frijolito never let them.

During our stretches, Frijolito would tell us about his big idea. "Jordan Cleats" He would go on and on about how he would buy some cleats if they were "Jordan." He was obsessed with that idea. The whole team would tell him to shut up, and he would laugh.

One time we had one game during the rain. I don't recall whether we won or lost, but I remember having fun. I remember getting home all muddy and my mom absolutely losing it. I think that will forever be my favorite game.

After our games, my mom would take us home. And whether she worked or not, would decide what we did. If my mom was home, we would stay in and play video games. If my mom was at work, we would roam the neighborhood.

We always made sure to get back home before my mom returned home.

After dinner, we would go into my room and spend the night talking. We would talk about anything and everything. Sometimes we talked about what girls were cute. We both liked the twins, and in my mind we could even date them, but we liked the same one. Even though they were identical, Ceanna was prettier than Celestina. Something about her two dimples.

Other times we would have serious talks where we shared secrets. That's when I learned he had lost an academic year when he came from Mexico.

I realized he was a whole year older than me.

Frijolito had an array of ghost stories he would share with me.

He swore he would be awoken in the middle of the night at the sound of hooves at a distance. Growing louder and louder, like they were approaching him. It would be followed by a light breeze, but when he opened his window to see what was outside, whatever was out there would disappear.

He even knew what houses were haunted in his old neighborhood or as he would say, "Espantan"[53]. He always knew the origin of the hauntings. They all included tragic tales of death. While other times it was due to witches that had practiced dark magic.

He had so many stories to tell, but my favorite one happened to his dad, or he claimed it did.

"So, my dad was driving home," he began. "He was in another city. I don't recall why he was there, but se le hizo tarde. It was late, but he wanted to get home as soon as possible. He was warned that it was dangerous since it was dark and getting cloudy. That meant that visibility was limited since it was through a mountain range and the moon was covered. Regrettably, he ignored them and decided to drive home.

But before he left, he was blessed and wished for a safe passage. Unfortunately, as soon as he left, it began to pour. It was raining hard, so he had to be extra careful because the road was full of potholes.

Besides dealing with the constant rain, he said most of the ride was normal. Nothing crazy, but somewhere between his destination, something caught his eye in the distance. He couldn't make out what it was.

---

[53] Haunted

Once he got closer, he recognized it was a couple. He became cautious and considered driving past them, but he couldn't leave them stranded. So, he pulled over and let them in.

My dad described them as an older couple once they were in the car, maybe around their 60s. Even though they had been out in the rain, they were surprisingly dry and were dressed in all-white. The man had on a white button-up shirt that was fairly ironed. With some white pants, a tan belt, and some tan boots. As for his wife, she had on an elegant white nightgown, but he didn't get a look at what else she was wearing.

As he drove, mi apa was somewhat spooked and nervous but tried to calm himself. They both sat in the back seat, and he tried to make small talk.

He asked for their names, but he's terrible at remembering them, so he doesn't recall them. He does remember asking them what they were doing out here in the middle of the night. Since there were no houses or anything for kilometers, but he hit a pothole before they got the chance to answer.

He lost control of the car and drove off the edge. There was nothing he could do, so he just braced for the impact. As he was rolling down the side of a mountain. My dad described it like it was all happening in slow motion. He said that he caught a glimpse of them through his rear-view mirror as they were rolling. He said his mysterious passengers looked calm and peaceful. Then he felt the final tumble at the bottom of the mountain. My dad was shocked and felt the adrenaline running through his body. He took his seatbelt off, got out of the vehicle, and realized he had no scratches on him. He was completely unharmed. It was unbelievable.

His car was completely totaled, but he was okay. So, he decided to check on his passengers, but there was no sign of them. It was like they had never existed. A passing car later picked up my dad, but he stood out there for hours. He was cold and wet, but he was alive. He later went to pick up the car and assess the damage, but he never got the answer to what happened to his passengers."

This is what my weekends would consist of; I absolutely loved it. Just hearing stories while I was wrapped up in my Mexican blanket, you know the one with the tiger on it.

That was until we started going to church on Sunday mornings.

El San Frijolito

Since school was ending and summer vacation was approaching, my mom was more relaxed about the sleepovers. Frijolito and I convinced my mom and his parents to let Frijolito sleep over on a Sunday.

I asked his parents, and he asked my mom since it's more difficult for parents to say no to children that aren't theirs. Of course, my mom was hesitant, but we promised to wake early and walk to school the next day. My mom caved and agreed. We even promised Frijolito's parents that we would go to misa.

Early that Sunday morning, we kept our promise and went to church. I had never gone to church consistently, so it would be a new experience.

We had breakfast and got ready. I noticed that Frijolito had a gold chain. It was thin, but it had a polished pendant at the bottom. I had seen her image before. It was the, "Virgen María"[54].

Since my mom had worked at night and was still asleep, we had to walk to church. His dad and older brother had to work so they wouldn't be there. Also, his mom and sister had already gone to the earlier session.

We got there right on time, so that meant that we had to sit in the back. I could tell that Frijolito didn't like sitting in the back. He complained that he could barely hear and that he couldn't see the priest.

Going to church was comprised a lot of standing, sitting, and kneeling.

I hated church.

---

[54] Virgen Mary

Frijolito took mass more seriously than me. He had gone through all the religious steps. He had been baptized and gone through confirmation.

I had no idea if I had even been baptized.

I went through the songbook and tried to read it, hoping it would entertain me. It was no use. I could feel myself falling back asleep.

I tried to tell a joke to Frijolito, to have him mess around. But he wasn't having it. He was serious. It was the first time I saw him take anything seriously. He followed what everybody did. He knew all the songs and prayers. As I tried to joke once again, a lady behind us tapped me on the shoulder and "shushed me".

I ignored her and tried to laugh it off, but I saw in Frijolito's face that he was in no mood to laugh or joke about anything. This was important to him.

I felt embarrassed. My mom had never pushed religion on me, so I didn't fully understand how significant this was to people. I figured church was something important to Mexicans.

El Hielo

As we walked home, I felt ashamed, but Frijolito seemed to be over it. He was more concerned with eating. When we arrived home, we went into the kitchen to see what we could make for lunch.

I went into the cabinets and found some Maruchan cups. Frijolito just stared at me and opened the fridge. My mom woke up and offered to make us lunch. Frijolito declined and insisted that he knew how to cook.

He asked my mom if we could use anything inside the fridge. She had no problems with that, and he began prepping vegetables to make us all fried chicken.

While he cooked, I didn't know what to do, so I tried helping him as much as possible but found myself mostly interfering with his work. All while my mom judged me with her stare.

The food turned out great, and he offered to wash the dishes once we finished eating. My mom couldn't let that happen.

So instead, he asked my mom if she wanted us to clean the backyard. She looked at me and, with delight, said, "Me encantaría"[55].

I had never done yard work or fixed anything around the house. I had never even held a shovel or a hammer before.

I was pretty annoyed. I had not signed up for any of this. We were both wasting a perfectly good Sunday on this. Working in the sun, and we weren't even going to get paid.

Midway through, my mom brought us lemonade she had just made. Since I was thirsty, I chugged mine right away, but I heard Frijolito say, "Gracias" before he sipped on his.

---

[55] I'd love that.

"Malcriado,"[56] I heard my mom say as she walked away. Now I was getting irritated. After being outside in the heat for a couple of hours, I was all sweaty and sticky. I tried to ignore Frijolito and began chewing on the ice left in the cup. This puzzled Frijolito, and he asked me if it didn't hurt my teeth.

I shook my head, and we continued working in silence. I was mad at Frijolito, but he was just being nice. I guess I started feeling jealous of him. After raking the grass into piles, he went to the side of the house and found an old shovel.

I told him, "Honestly, I didn't even know we had a shovel here."

"I don't think you even knew that shovels existed," he responded as he laughed.

The backyard had not looked this clean since we moved in. Even though I was feeling a type of way, it did feel nice to work with my hands.

Once inside, I wanted to lie on my bed, but my mom told me we had to shower first. I was feeling too lazy, but I knew she was right.

We both took turns showering and got ready for dinner. My mom had dinner ready for us, and as we ate, she got ready for work. She was still on the night schedule.

As she was leaving, we promised that we wouldn't stay up late and kissed her goodbye. Frijolito la persigno[57], which was weird, but it would have been even more bizarre if he kissed her on the cheek.

So, it would be just the two of us, but I was too tired to get into any type of trouble. As much as I hated it, I was impressed with Frijolito's cooking and working skills.

I asked him if his dad had taught him how to do yard work. He nodded and said, "My brother and I both go work with him during the summers," he said.

It was the first time he mentioned his brother.

---

[56] Spoiled
[57] Make the sign of the holy cross.

"You don't go to Mexico during your summers?" I asked.

"No puedo," he responded, "They won't let me come back."

"Who's they?" I asked.

"La migra,"[58], he responded.

I didn't quite understand what he was saying, but I didn't ask any more questions.

We continued watching T.V. for a few minutes and decided it was time to sleep.

We both lay in my room with the lights off. It took our eyes a while to adjust to the darkness.

It was quiet, and I don't know if it was just because we were tired from all the work we had done or if we had finally run out of things to talk about.

Frijolito broke the silence and asked, "Do you remember your first day of school?"

"Yeah?" I answered, confused, and began wondering where this conversation was heading.

"Do you remember Paulino?"

"Not really."

"He was the kid that bumped into you and kicked your schedule."

"You saw that?" I asked him.

"Yeah," he said with a pause.

"Well, I didn't like how he did that to you, anyways a few days later I was walking to class. My parents had just bought me some brand-new Nikes. I rarely get new shoes, so I like to take care of them. Anyways, I don't know why but Paulino made fun of my shoes and stepped on them as he walked away with his little crew. That pissed me off, so I waited for him to be alone in the restroom during lunch. When he finally went to the bathroom, I ran in there after him, and when he noticed me in there with him, I could tell he was scared. I knew we were going to fight, so I socked him in his mouth, but he didn't do anything. He was just

---

[58] U.S. Immigration and Customs Enforcement

standing there. I felt terrible but was still angry, so I punched him again. And I told him that the first one was for my shoes and the second was for Xavi. So, De nada." He finished in a sarcastic tone.

"Eres un buen amigo,"[59] I said as I laughed, "Is that why your hands were red and why you were late to music class."

"I don't know, I don't remember what day that was. I got ISS or something, I think."

We both laughed; I guess I remembered that day differently. It was the day I cheated on the quiz. He didn't get ISS because of the fight; he got it because of me. I wanted to say something, but it got quiet once again. I missed my opportunity to own up to it.

Then out of nowhere, we heard a noise outside in the backyard.

We didn't know what was going on. We saw a shadow back there. Unable to see what it was, I realized it was a person. We made eye contact, and then he took off. I looked at Frijolito, and he stared back at me. We both froze up.

There was a loud knock on the front door. We both ran to the door and saw red and blue flashing lights. It was blinding.

I opened the door, and a man with a uniform and flashlight asked us if we had seen anybody coming through. I nodded and mentioned the man we saw in our backyard. He tried to grab us both and asked if anybody else was in the house.

"No," I said.

I was being compliant.

Frijolito had been frozen this whole time. He looked at me and ran towards my room. I ran in after him, and the officer yelled at us to come outside. We didn't listen. I just ran after Frijolito.

I found Frijolito in my room, hiding under my lion blanket. We didn't say anything. It was quiet, besides his

---

[59] You're a good friend.

heavy breathing. I didn't know this at that time, but he was having a panic attack.

The whole neighborhood was blocked off, and after an hour, it was all over. They caught the man they were looking for. Everything was quiet and back to normal again, but the damage was done.

I asked Frijolito if he was okay.

He didn't answer and asked me if I knew who they were.

I shook my head.

"La migra," he said softly.

I didn't know who they were, and I had never been afraid of I.C.E. agents before.

The truth is I didn't know much about them, I had seen them driving on the freeway, but I never had to interact with them.

I didn't understand what made Border Patrol scary.

As we tried getting some sleep that night, I thought about how Frijolito had taught me how to use a shovel that day, but I also learned what privilege was, even though I didn't have the word for it.

My Mom's Homecoming

As school came to an end, I told Frijolito that our adventures would be placed on hold. I was going to Mexico for the summer. I had not been to Mexico in a while, but my mom had recently received her green card. After being stuck in the United States for twelve years, she could finally go to Mexico.

When I was younger, I vaguely remember we had to take a bus to meet a lawyer. My mom had to talk to her and apply for residency through her work. She was granted a work permit but still had to go through interviews, approvals, rejections, and loads of paperwork. All in a span of twelve years.

My mom had been saving all her vacation days in hopes that one day she would be granted permission to return home.

I had not been to Mexico in what felt like forever, but I bet she felt it had been even longer for her. She couldn't hold her excitement as we packed our car and drove away.

It was a 9-hour drive, so we got there late at night. After stopping for gas, snacks, and frequent bathroom breaks, we made it.

My family lived in a small ranch town near Campo Dulce, Sonora. We had to get off the main road and turn onto a dirt road to get there. There weren't many streetlights, and it was awfully quiet.

When we arrived, everybody was still awake. Anticipating our arrival, well, mostly for my mom, some of my uncles and aunts had not seen my mom in years. Neither had my grandpa or grandma. They did talk on the phone often, but it was not the same.

They were all overwhelmed with tears. I couldn't grasp the importance of this moment. Then it turned into a celebration.

As late as it was, I couldn't believe they had waited for us.

I was overwhelmed by the number of hugs and kisses I received. Then I saw my grandpa go behind the cupboard and grab an old dark glass bottle. I didn't know what it was, it was still pretty full, and he poured dark golden liquid into a small glass cup.

"What's that?" I asked.

Everybody in the room froze and looked at me; I forgot I couldn't speak English here. Nobody here understood me, and I felt embarrassed.

"Es tequila," said my mom.

"Pero del bueno,"[60] added my grandpa.

As she drank the golden liquid, her face puckered up. I could tell she had regretted drinking it. Her face said disgusted, but everyone around her cheered.

My grandpa also took a shot, but he didn't make any faces. He looked at the bottle and hid it once again.

I turned around and saw a fraction of my entire family standing in the living room, looking back at me. I hadn't talked to or seen them in years. It felt surreal being with so many relatives in one place. I couldn't focus on any of them.

Then I recognized my grandma, and I was instantly filled with joy. I didn't realize how much I had missed her. She was the only one sitting in her rocking chair. She was waiting for me to go up and hug her, but not before she hugged my mom tightly. She had already waited years to see my mom and couldn't wait any longer.

My grandma pointed out how much I had grown.

"Pues claro eras un bebe cuando te fuiste."[61], she said.

"¿Todavía te meas?"[62], asked somebody in the crowd.

---

[60] The good kind.
[61] Of course, he was just a baby when he left.
[62] You still wet the bed?

Well, no, I was a baby when I left. I think. I don't
remember how young I was, I thought.

My grandma just smiled at me. I could see she had
missed her youngest daughter. She told us to sit down and
have dinner. Nobody else ate since they had already eaten.
I heard her turn on the gas stove, unsure what we would
be eating. To my surprise, it was chorizo. I was glad it
wasn't nopales or some other weird food. I thought about
sitting down. But my mom looked at me and said, "Saluda.
¿Qué no te enseñan eso en la escuela?"[63]

There was a large misconception between what my mom
thought they taught in schools and what I actually learned
there.

I ignored my hunger and went around saying hello to
everybody there, as I tried to recognize people or even
remember their names. I couldn't. Everybody knew who I
was, but I had no clue who they were.

Then a couple of my cousins and uncles called me a
"Gringo"[64]. I had never been called that before. I felt out of
place. I wasn't white, so why would they call me a "Gringo".
I sometimes felt too Mexican before, but this was the first
time I felt too American.

"¿Tienes a una guerita?"[65] I heard somebody ask me.

"No," I said.

"Es que no eres hombre, te van a hacer quinceañera,
¿verdad?"[66]

Everybody in the room made a face like I had been
disrespected or something. I didn't understand what was
happening.

I'm just in middle school, and what's a quinceañera, I
thought.

---

[63] Introduce yourself, don't they teach you that at school?

[64] The term for a foreigner, often a Euro-American, but can also be
used for somebody who is out of touch with their culture.

[65] Do you have a blonde girlfriend?

[66] It's because he's not a man. You're going to have a quinceañera
aren't you?

Noriega

I just sat down and ate my food quietly. *I wish Frijolito was here*, I thought, *he would know what to do.*

After hours of talking and catching up, everybody eventually went home. By this time, I had already fallen asleep.

My Mexican Summer

The next couple of days, my mom forced me to go with her. I had to meet different people from her past life. Old friends and distant relatives.

When we got into a car, I realized that seatbelts were optional. It was also the first time I rode in the back of a truck. I couldn't hold on to anything and kept sliding all over the place. The hard metal frame was uncomfortable, and I had no room inside.

This is awfully dangerous, I thought, but nobody else seemed to care.

That was the beginning of my summer. The rest of it was filled with running outside all day. Asking my mom for a dollar and going to "las tienditas"[67], playing soccer "Retas"[68] in the cement courts, and spending pesos in the "Maquinitas"[69]. This was very different than going to the pool and watching television all day.

My life began to revolve around which novelas[70] were on. My whole family would sit in front of this antique television. Not high definition by any means, and just watch whatever new episode was out. Unless it rained, because then all the power lines would be down.

I loved the rain, but my grandma was always superstitious. She would say that I couldn't play in the rain. She would remind me not to be under large trees or to touch anything metal. I couldn't shower either because I was told I could get hit with a lightning bolt.

---

[67] Store
[68] Pick-up games
[69] Arcade games
[70] Soap Operas

I understood why not everybody loved the rain when I saw the damage it could do. I would see trees fall, houses lose part of their roofs and hear about children getting swept by the water.

But, I would see rivers form. I would get the chills whenever I heard thunder, and I loved seeing the whole landscape turn green overnight. My grandma taught me that plants grew better because rainwater was the best type of water.

Before that summer, I had no idea who "El Chavo" was, but I instantly appreciated him. After watching all their movies, I grew to respect "Cantinflas" and "La India María." I mean, that is pretty much all they would play in the two channels we had. There was a whole side of television I had never experienced before. They both spoke humorously, but it was not demeaning. It was funnier than I had expected it to be.

I mean, there were some similarities. I would have to wake up early on the weekends to watch tv, but it wasn't to watch cartoons. It was to watch "El Chabelo." It wasn't the same as watching cartoons, but it entertained me all the same.

All these actors were old. But somehow they entertained me.

Before having to leave back to work, my mom left me a couple of dollars and told me I would have to make them last until the end of summer. I considered going with her, but I wanted to stay. There was so much to explore, and I wanted to spend time with my family. I had not been away from my mom since I was a baby, but I had no recollection of those days.

I was pretty sad seeing my mom go. One of my cousins noticed I was down when I said goodbye.

He began picking on me and started to say, "Quiere llorar pero no puede."[71]

---

[71] He wants to cry but he can't.

That didn't make any sense, I did want to cry, and I just had to hold it back. I didn't understand why I couldn't express my sadness. I had always been okay with being sad, but I learned I was no longer allowed to.

Since my mom had left me, I had to rely on my grandma for everything. Which was great because I loved my grandma's cooking. I especially loved it when she would make tortillas. She would make them over a fire outside and sometimes asked me if I wanted to help. I always wanted to help, but honestly, my tortillas were terrible.

Something about those tortillas with butter hit differently.

Every afternoon my cousins and I would go play soccer on these courts made out of cement. I had always been used to playing in the grass and dirt, but it didn't matter. I would still end up with the same scraped knees.

Even though I considered myself Mexican, not everybody felt the same about me.

One day during one of our trips to the local plaza. I saw a group of kids approaching me. They knew that I wasn't from here. I didn't know how or why because, in my eyes, I was just like them, but somehow, they knew that I was different. They started asking me questions, like where I was from. I didn't know what to say. I didn't want to say I was an American because it felt wrong.

One spoke up and asked, "¿Eres del otro lado?"[72]

I knew what that meant but didn't want to answer. It wasn't that I was ashamed, but I was scared. I was scared of being deported. It didn't work that way, but I didn't know that back then, so I just stayed quiet.

I just avoided them from that day on.

Every Sunday, my whole family would go to the local river. We would all pack up and ride in somebody's pickup truck. Before we left, we would always stop at an "Expendio"[73]. You could find all types of snacks there, but

---

[72] Are you from the other side of the border?

[73] Small beer shop

my uncles would just buy beer. Sometimes if we were lucky, we would get a bag of chips to split among the thirty children. We didn't mind, though; we loved going to the river. There were other families, all enjoying the water and just taking in the day. Sundays at the river, I knew I would miss this the most.

This was my routine for the whole summer. And even though I loved it, just like all things, it would come to an end.

As sad as it was, summer was over. It was time to go home. Something about leaving made me emotional; I didn't want to say bye to my grandma, but I had to. I did cry a little. She just joked about how I was leaving darker than how I had arrived. I kissed her goodbye.

Well, that's how it started. I had to kiss her on the cheek first. Then I had to go around and give one to all my aunts and hugs to my uncles. All my cousins too. Basically, the whole block, after 30 minutes, I was finished. So, then I decided to give my grandma another kiss. Man, saying goodbye was not only sad, but it was also exhausting.

My mom's brother, my tío Armando, was taking me back home since my mom had already left. He only had a permit, no green card or anything like that.

But he had a full truck since he was transporting other people. Which meant that I had to sit in the bed of the truck, but that had become normal at this point.

I just remember waving goodbye to everybody. I waved for as long as I could until I could no longer see them, and they were gone entirely. The best part about riding in the back was that nobody could see me crying. This was the only place I could cry peacefully.

El Butterfinger

As we drove, I noticed so many little towns. Each one of them comes with a different set of speed bumps. Seeing people waving various goods in hopes that passing vehicles would buy some. Then some wanted to hitch a ride to go on further north. We didn't stop for either. We just stopped at an "OXXO" before leaving, and all I got was water.

After a couple of hours of driving in the back of the truck. My face began to feel weird. Like if there was a force field surrounding it. I wondered what that was and why my face was feeling this way.

We made one last stop when we were getting close to the border. My uncle opened the door, and all the passengers got off. They were going to cross the border walking. Only my uncle and I would cross in the car. Even though it wasn't sunny outside, my uncle, Armando, wanted me to sit inside.

"Es ilegal,"[74] he told me.

I listened to him, climbed out of the truck bed, and sat in the front. I even clicked my seatbelt on.

We kept getting approached by people who were selling small artisanal gifts. Little crosses, bracelets, wallets, and an extensive range of items. There were the occasional beggars that we would see. Some of them were disabled, others claimed they had recently been deported.

My uncle would just say, "Ahorita no,"[75] unfazed by whoever approached him.

Then this lady with various fruits mixed with chile and limón walked by. It made my mouth water as I saw the mangos, watermelons. jicama, oranges, and pineapples are all cut up and ready to be sold. Then we saw duros with

---

[74] It's illegal.
[75] Not right now.

chamoy. It was like I was walking through a snack shop. Of course, my uncle didn't offer me anything, and I didn't want to ask. It was not something I was comfortable with.

I asked him how long the line usually took.

"Dos o tres horas, a veces más,"[76] he responded.

Two or three hours or more of just sitting here with nothing to do. Nothing to snack on, I felt myself getting an urge to get out of the car and walk. I didn't want to be in the car anymore. I began feeling closed in and could feel myself starting to fidget. My tío noticed but didn't say anything.

An hour passed. I was at my breaking point. I looked at my uncle, and I felt him tense up. I looked up to see what he was looking at. It saw a white SUV on the local road trying to merge in. Not only was this car holding up traffic, but they were also trying to bypass the line and cut ahead. I could feel my uncle getting frustrated.

To our luck, a Mexican police officer approached the vehicle. We couldn't hear what was happening but could tell they were arguing.

My uncle looked at me and said, "Se me hace no que no se entienden."[77]

Before he said anything, I knew he would expect me, with my middle school English to resolve this diplomatic problem.

As I approached the SUV, I went up to the police officer. We made eye contact, and I nodded downwards at him. I introduced myself and explained that I knew both English and Spanish, so I could translate.

The SUV had its windows up, and a white lady was driving. I waved at her, but she completely ignored me. She looked away and pretended to be busy. I knocked on her window, and she rolled it down.

Before I could get a word out, she said,

"I don't have any money," and started reaching through her car.

---

[76] 2 or 3 hours, sometimes more.
[77] I don't think they can understand each other.

61

After a few seconds, she reached out and gave me a Butterfinger chocolate bar.

"Here you go, gracias," she said in an American accent.

I just stood there confused. I didn't know what to do.

I looked at the officer, who understood I was just as useless as him in this interaction.

I decided to keep the Butterfinger, I mean, it wasn't my favorite, but it was all I had to snack on.

The officer had enough and decided to get in front of the car. He aggressively motioned to her to get out of the line and go to the back. She then went ahead to put her middle finger up and drove away. I don't think the police officer needed me to translate that.

I walked back to my uncle's truck, chocolate in hand. As I closed the door, my uncle had the audacity to ask me for the chocolate. Can you believe that?

He asked me if that was my reward for translating. I told him I didn't even get a chance to say anything. That she had just ignored me and handed the chocolate bar to me.

My uncle started laughing.

I asked him why he was laughing, and he told me the lady probably thought I was a beggar. That I wanted money, and she probably felt bad for me.

"Le dio lastima,"[78] he said.

I felt humiliated. *I'm not a beggar*, I thought, *I never have been.*

I handed my uncle the chocolate. Then I realized she just saw me as a brown kid in Mexico. She was the only one that didn't see me as American. She saw me as a poor Mexican beggar.

I looked at my uncle, but he was eating my Butterfinger without a care in the world.

For the rest of the wait, I just sat there quietly.

After another hour, we were through. We went to a McDonalds. Still no food while we waited for everybody

---

[78] She felt sorry for you.

who had crossed walking to meet up. Those who crossed on foot took an extra hour.

After waiting an hour, we were all reunited. I was sent to the back, and we continued on our trip.

The sun was going down, but I knew we would have sunlight for another hour or so. Without anything to do, I looked at the horizon to see if I could find something to entertain me. I didn't see much, just a bunch of saguaros and mountains that didn't get any bigger or smaller.

That ended pretty fast, then after a couple of minutes, I heard a semi-truck honk at me. I looked up and saw the driver waving. He was so excited to see me. After that, every semi-truck I saw, I would motion to them to honk, and they all would. This made my drive slightly less irritating and much more exciting.

Then I saw an SUV approaching fast. They were speeding, merging in and out of traffic. Before driving past us, I made eye contact with the driver. It was the same lady from earlier.

What were the odds of that?

I looked at her, and she noticed me. I waved at her, but she didn't seem happy to see me. Instead of waving back, she flipped me off. I liked the Butterfinger more than this kind of finger. I didn't know what I had done to her to be treated like this. She must have still been upset about the incident earlier.

Or maybe not, I thought, *Maybe this lady is racist.*

I mean, I didn't know much about racism, but I did feel discriminated against.

As she drove away, I couldn't help but wonder about her. Then I realized that even on this side of the border, she still saw me as just another Mexican kid.

La Lotería

When I arrived home, my mom was waiting for me; it was late at night. I could tell she was exhausted but wanted to ensure I was home safely. We thanked my uncle as he left. He had other people to drop off.

I told my mom I wanted to see Frijolito. She just looked at me like I was crazy. It was too late for that and told me I had a whole week to hang out with him before school started.

She had a point, but I missed my best friend so much. Well, not enough to go to church with him the next day. I decided to go to his house after church was over.

My mom had work, so I had to walk to his house.

It wasn't a long walk, but after a few minutes, I was approaching the trailer park. I could hear my footsteps on the gravel, and when I saw his house, I noticed a bunch of cars outside parked along the side. I wondered what they were all doing here. Then I saw Frijolito and ran towards him, but then I stopped.

I noticed that there were a lot of people by his trailer. It felt like his whole family was there, grilling carne asada, sitting on the patio. The music was blasting on some old staticky speakers, and everybody seemed to be having a good time. I had never been to a party in the middle of the day, especially not on a Sunday.

I was not expecting to see so many people. I felt out of place.

I didn't know what to say. We hadn't talked in weeks, but I could tell he missed me as much as I had missed him.

"Es mi amigo Xavi,"[79] he said as he introduced me to everybody.

---

[79] It's my friend Xavier.

I introduced myself to all his aunts, uncles, and cousins. This was something I was familiar with.

He noticed that I had gotten darker and taller, but he was still the same Frijolito.

He walked me to a chair and sat me down. Before I could react to anything, there was a plate of food on my lap. There was carne asada, cebolla, limones, frijoles. It was a full meal.

After a while, we began talking about our summers. His days were filled with work, but he had way more stories to tell than I did.

He even mentioned that he had learned how to drive. "Estándar,"[80] he said.

I don't know what that meant. I was nowhere near getting my driver's permit, so the idea of learning how to drive seemed distant.

Frijolito's family was loud. All the uncles were on the side, drinking beer, grilling more food, and laughing.

Then somebody pulled out a stack of cards, and everybody began fighting for one.

"What is this?" I asked.

"La Lotería."[81], he told me.

I saw people scrambling to get loose change from their cars and a good seat at the table.

Then the game started, and I heard words shouted, "El Corazón, La Mano, El Diablo, La Calavera..."

People were throwing pieces of uncooked beans onto the boards.

"Lotería!" I heard somebody yell, and everybody else groaned.

All this was over a couple of dollars; I wanted to play but had no money. Thankfully, Frijolito covered for me.

It was nice to be back.

Midway through the game, I noticed a girl come outside from the trailer. I looked at her, and before I could even

---

[80] Standard

[81] A traditional game of chance, sometimes called Mexican Bingo.

finish a thought, Frijolito looked at me and said, "Ni lo pienses, es mi hermana."[82] As he continued to focus on his board.

He had never mentioned her, but from the looks of it, he was very protective of her. I respected him, so I cleared my head.

A couple of hours later, my mom picked me up and took me home.

"Why don't we do stuff like this?" I asked her.

"¿Como qué?"[83] she asked?

"Jugar a la Lotería,"[84] I said.

"You want to play Lotería with me?" She asked.

Then I remembered that it was just us two. It had always been just the two of us.

---

[82] Don't even think about it, that's my sister.
[83] Like what?
[84] Like playing board games.

El Río Amacuzac

Seeing that I still had a week. I decided to spend most of that time with Frijolito. My past summers had been filled with watching reruns and staying trapped indoors. I wanted this to be different. He slept over the whole week. I didn't mind. I guess my mom was happy seeing that I had a friend come around.

That week Frijolito didn't have to work. I tried my best to keep him entertained and hoped he wouldn't want to return home out of boredom. We did some yard work the first couple of days, but there was only so much we could do around the house.

I tried to get him to play more video games, but that only entertained him for a bit.

I wanted to play soccer outside, but it was just too hot outside to play anything. Our local park had a pool.

I told Frijolito we should go to the pool, but he just brushed it off.

When I first brought it up, he said, "No."

He was skeptical, but I tried to convince him to join me. We searched through the house, looking for my pants.

But I kept bugging him again and again. I put my hand on his shoulder and pulled it towards and away from me.

"Andale," I said, "Di que si."[85]

Sometimes, being annoying convinced my mom, so maybe it would work on him too.

I was getting to him when he said, "I didn't bring anything to swim in."

I told him that I had clothes for him.

He responded, "Your shorts are too small for me."

"We wear the same size shorts."

---

[85] "Come on, say yes."

"Yeah, but my legs are thicker than your chicken legs."

"Since when do you check out my legs?" I asked.

I could see him thinking, trying to come up with something to say, but he remained silent.

"Vamos pues,"[86] I said while packing a bag with towels and sunscreen.

I could tell he didn't want to go but tagged along. He knew that if he didn't go, I would never let him forget.

We had to pay a couple of dollars to get in when we got there.

"No tengo feria,"[87] he said as he hit his pockets, pretending to look for money.

"Lo que me gané de la Lotería,"[88] I told him as I pulled out just enough money to cover our entrance.

This might come to you as a surprise, but Frijolito didn't know how to swim. I didn't know that. That was until he confessed to me before we left the lockers.

"It's easy."

"How did you learn?"

I stood there for a second, trying to recollect that specific memory. I was flooded with other random thoughts; *Did I take the chicken out of the freezer? Did I lock the front door? Remember when you fell while running down the stairs at school, and that 1st grader saw you? Do you remember where you put your passport? What about swimming?*

I looked at him, but I couldn't remember.

"When did I learn how to swim? Do I even know how to swim?" I questioned myself.

"I was pushed in, and I had to learn."

He looked at me, he didn't say anything, but his eyes said, "Ni que se te ocurra."[89]

---

[86] Let's go.

[87] I don't have any money.

[88] This is what I won from Lotería.

[89] Don't even think about it.

I mean, he was physically bigger than me. I couldn't physically push him unless I did it by surprise, but it wasn't something I considered doing.

We went outside and saw some kids from school. He covered up and said he was just going to sit on one of the chairs with his shirt on.

"No empieces,[90] we came all this way to come swim."

"Me da verguenza."[91]

"Bro, you rather be 13 and not know how to swim or be 30?"

"I'm 14," he corrected me, "and I rather not drown."

"Look, there are lifeguards here. If you start to drown, I'll tell one of the cute ones to rescue you."

"Which one?"

"La que tú quieras,"[92] I said.

"Esa," he said, pointing to a lifeguard with just lifting his eyebrows.

I didn't even look in that direction, *I hope it's the dude that has to rescue him, I thought, laughing.*

He took off his shirt and stepped in. I don't know why, but Frijolito thought he was walking in through the shallow end for some reason. He was not. He just walked into the deep end. Unaware of what he had done, he started panicking. As soon as he hit the water, he sank like a rock. Luckily, he was close enough to the edge for me to grab him. I reached in and grabbed him. He was too heavy for me to pull him out by myself. So, he helped me.

Once out of the pool, he caught his breath and looked at me.

"Me estaba ahogando."[93]

"I saw that."

He walked away from the pool. He was not happy with me. He told me he didn't want to go in anymore.

---

[90] Don't even start,
[91] I'm embarrassed.
[92] Whichever one you want.
[93] I was drowning.

"Porque no eres hombre,"[94] I said. That got to him. Every Mexican's kryptonite. There is something fragile about a Mexican man's masculinity that could easily be manipulated if you just attack their manliness, or so I had learned. This could explain why so many Mexican men are machista.

Frijolito turned around and ran towards the pool. I was trying to call his bluff, but he jumped in feet first.

It was so stupid. He wasn't close enough to reach the ledge and looked like he was drowning. I instantly regretted saying that to him. I started to run, and I looked back at him. Before I could yell for help, he swam back to the edge.

He laughed at me. I was too relieved to care that he had deceived me.

"¿Sabés nadar?"[95]

"¿Qué no me vez? Ciego."[96]

"¿Dónde Aprendiste?"[97]

"En un rio haya en Morelos."[98]

I could tell from his voice was getting excited.

"En el Rio Amacuzac. Estaba a una hora de mi casa. Cada año íbamos en Semana Santa. Hay un montón de cascadas donde caía el agua. El Rio esta grande. Y si no sabes nadar te lleva la corriente y te pierdes. Todo alrededor está bien verde, así como tú. La verdad es lo más bonito que hay en el mundo."[99]

I tried to picture the river where he grew up. I had never seen a waterfall or been in a place like that.

"Then why didn't you want to swim?"

---

[94] Because you're not a man.
[95] You know how to swim?
[96] Can't you see? Are you blind?
[97] Where did you learn?
[98] In a river out in Morelos.
[99] The Amacuzac river was an hour away from our home. We would go every year during our spring break. It had multiple waterfalls, and the river was huge, but the currents were strong so if you don't know how to swim you'd disappear. The whole landscape is green, it is the most beautiful place on earth.

Noriega

He just shrugged, and with a sad tone, he said, "I guess it makes me miss back home."

"This is your home," I replied.

"No, this is where I live, but this will never be my home."

I didn't say anything. I just sat there thinking about all the Mexicans that lived here but would rather be back home.

I wondered if my mom was one of those Mexicans.

Music Taste

I didn't want to go to the pool for the rest of the week, but I didn't want us to die of boredom. I thought about what we could do. Frijolito asked me if I knew how to download music.

I had never downloaded music before.

"Yeah," he said, "We can create a playlist."

I had forgotten how much of a music freak he was.

"Sure."

I got on my mom's laptop but didn't know where to go.

I typed "Download Music," and it took me to a website.

All I had to do was paste a link here, and it would get the song of my choice. That seemed pretty straightforward. Maybe a little bit too easy. I didn't know what else to do, but it seemed good enough for Frijolito.

We both took turns searching for songs and discussing whether we liked them. I quickly realized that most of his songs were what my uncles listened to when they drank around my grandma's house.

"There is nothing wrong with Mexican music. I just don't like it," I said.

Frijolito quickly turned to me and looked offended.

"You know there is more than one type of Mexican music genre."

"What's a genre? All Mexican music is the same."

Frijolito started counting on his hand as he said," Hay mariachi, ranchera, norteño, banda, corridos, rock, narcocorridos, cumbias, conjuntos, y muchas más."

I thought about what I was going to say. I had grown up listening to Rap and Hip-Hop music. I wondered at what age a person developed a preference in music.

Noriega

Frijolito stopped searching for songs and instead looked at my list. He scrolled down and realized that none of the songs I downloaded were Mexican or in Spanish.

"No tienes ninguna canción en español."[100]

"Si mira esta," I replied.

"He's not even Mexican; he's Boricua,"[101] he said.

"What's that?"

"Que es de Puerto-Rico, no sabes nada de Latinoamérica."[102]

I was afraid to ask more questions, so it got quiet.

"Ni eres mexicano tú,"[103] he finished.

Now it was me that was offended. He was right. I didn't have anything he had in terms of Mexican culture in my life. I only spoke Spanish because of my mom, and even then, we barely spoke it.

I looked at his playlist and tried remembering some of the songs he downloaded. "I have to like these songs," I told myself, "If I want to be Mexican."

---

[100] You don't even have any Spanish songs.
[101] Somebody that is from Puerto Rico or Puerto Rican descent.
[102] That he's from Puerto Rico, you don't know anything about Latin America.
[103] You're not even Mexican.

In a Pickle

The rest of the week flew by, and just like that, it was our last year in middle school, 8th grade. As for how our year went, it was pretty ordinary. Just me and Frijolito living life.

As for our weekends, they were still filled with Pancakes and soccer games. We still stayed up during the weekend and had our late-night talks. Our conversations evolved into more serious discussions, or we would just have arguments about dumb scenarios we created in our heads. This had become our new norm.

That was until we found a spare key to my mom's car.

I figured it was my turn to learn how to drive since Frijolito was already an experienced driver.

Frijolito volunteered to be my teacher, and once it was decided, we knew we had to go out somewhere.

We came up with a plan as I ate a pickle.

"Asco."[104]

Can you believe this dude's nerve? Calling me out for eating pickles when he likes nopales.

I ignored him.

The plan was simple: we would take my mom's car while she slept and just go for a cruise. Nothing crazy. No showing off, just us two going for a quick ride.

I don't know why it had never occurred to us before. We didn't need the spare. We could have easily just taken the actual keys since they were in a basket next to the door.

We decided it would be best if Frijolito drove us to a location, parked the car, and then I would drive back.

Pretty simple, actually.

---

[104] Gross

That night we snuck out through the back door and tried not to make any noise. We managed to escape without any incidents.

I hadn't been this excited about getting in a car since my younger days when my mom would take me to the Mexican store.

I could feel my heart racing, but I trusted Frijolito.

He put the key in the ignition, started the car, put it in reverse, and we were gone.

We drove for a few minutes until we came upon an empty street. There were no cars on the side of the road. Frijolito turned off the car and told me to switch seats. It was my turn to drive. I didn't know what to do with my pickle, so I told Frijolito to hold on to it. I had never sat in the driver's seat before. I had seen people drive before, but this was all foreign to me.

Frijolito tried his best to teach me how to drive. I listened carefully as he told me what every knob, pedal, and lever did. It was truly a learning experience.

"¿Listo?"[105] he asked.

I nodded nervously.

I shifted gears like he had told me and pressed the gas. The car made a lot of noise as I stepped on the gas, but it didn't go anywhere. It just started rolling backward. I looked over at Frijolito, confused.

"Esta en neutral,"[106] he said.

I could feel the car gaining speed in reverse.

"Manea, Manea,"[107] he yelled.

I didn't know what to do, but I saw we were heading straight toward a wall.

Out of panic, I stepped on a pedal, and the car came to a stop. The lights turned on inside of one of the houses. I didn't know what to do, so Frijolito put the car in drive for me. Again, I stepped on a pedal, and the car shot forward. I didn't

---

[105] Ready?
[106] It's in neutral.
[107] Brake. Brake.

know how to turn or what to do. I made a sharp turn and hit a mailbox.

This time I could hear people walking outside their homes to see what all the chaos was about. I put the car in park and thought about stopping. Frijolito grabbed me and switched seats. We drove off. I looked back and saw people in the middle of the road. I had never been in an accident before, especially not a hit-and-run.

We drove home, but you could hear us breathing hard before we got out of the car. I didn't know what to say.

I turned to Frijolito and asked him, "Where's my pickle?"

He smacked me in the back of the head and turned off the car. We both got off and inspected the damage. There wasn't much but a small scratch in the front. We both knew how lucky we had gotten. We walked back inside and decided to leave the driving lessons for another day.

Noriega

La Fiesta

A week later, Frijolito's sister was having a birthday party.

"Don't get any ideas about my sister," he reminded me.

I ran down to ask my mom, who was hesitant about me staying there too late. It was starting to sound like a "no." I signaled to Frijolito to come over.

"He could sleep over," He suggested.

My mom looked at me, defeated. She knew she couldn't say no.

I packed my soccer uniform, toothbrush, and clothes for the party.

My mom dropped us off, and I asked her where she was going. "A mandado,"[108] she said "Te portas bien."[109]

The invitation said 2:00 p.m., but it was already 3 in the afternoon, and nothing had been set up.

There was no sign of a party anywhere. I was assigned chair duty, so I had to put chairs at every table. As I did that, Frijolito's mom put colorful plastic coverings on the tables and some glass vases filled with water, pebbles, and flowers.

"Este es mi recuerdo,"[110] said one of the ladies already claiming it.

After that, we had to get the sodas into a cooler and make sure that there was plenty of ice to go with them. A much bigger cooler was next to it, but that one was for beer. I didn't understand why they needed so much beer.

The women walked around, ensuring every table had chips, salsa, a two-liter soda, and cups.

---

[108] Errands
[109] Behave yourself.
[110] Souvenir

The cake was at a table that had room for all the gifts. I remembered that I had not gotten a gift for her, and just then, I saw my mom pulling up.

"El regalo,"[111] she said, handing me the gift.

She said hi to everybody, Frijolito's parents asked her to stay, but she politely declined. She claimed that she had to go to work.

I would catch glimpses of Frijolito's sister, Sofia, but I tried hard not to stare. She was wearing a long dress and seemed excited about the party.

The music started blasting, and people began arriving. I didn't know anybody here besides Frijolito.

The party had officially started. So, I ran inside and got ready. The bathroom was occupied, so I went into Frijolito's room. It was small, with only one bed and no closet. I rushed to get ready and headed outside.

I sat down at a table and waited for the food. Food was coming out, but I ate alone. Frijolito was helping serve. Kids were running around. I heard music starting to blast and was nervous somebody would ask me to dance, nobody did, but that would have been embarrassing since I didn't know how to dance.

Frijolito sat down, and we began to talk. After we finished eating, we went with the other adult men. Honestly, it was so boring. I wanted to do anything else. Then men were on one side of the house, just drinking beer and talking about how hard work was. One would tell jokes, and everybody would laugh. I didn't understand the jokes, so I would just laugh.

When Sofia started to open gifts none of the men seemed to care. All the women sat around the table. I kept hearing oohing and aahing.

The men just kept drinking and talking. No matter how many beers they took out of the cooler, it wouldn't get empty.

---

[111] Gift

After the gifts, it was time for cake. It was honestly pretty late by this point. All the kids that had been running around were sleeping in chairs. I could feel myself getting tired.

Some people began to leave, and I figured that the party was coming to an end. I was wrong. It seemed like it was barely starting. The music got louder, and so did the drunks. You couldn't even understand what they were slurring.

Sofia saw me and could tell I was bored. She approached me, and we introduced ourselves officially, but before we could start conversing, Frijolito pulled me away. I was back to the boring talks.

Sofia decided to go to sleep. It was late, after all.

Frijolito had other plans, he wanted me to stay up late with him, and while his older brother, dad, and his uncles were distracted, he snuck a couple of beers from the cooler.

I was nervous. I didn't know what to do. I mean, I had never had a beer before.

"Vamos a tomar,"[112] he said.

We snuck to the back of the trailer, where nobody could see us. We opened it and started drinking. It didn't taste good. It was awful. That sip I had gotten was more than enough. We didn't finish a single can, but then Christian caught us.

"¿Qué están haciendo?"[113,] he asked.

"Nada," said Frijolito.

I had never seen him this nervous before. He was scared. I could see him shaking, and his voice started to crack.

"Si no se las toman todas, le voy a decir a mi apa,"[114] he threatened.

I didn't want to drink anymore, but now we had to.

Frijolito and I looked at each other, and both started drinking. After we finished, I instantly felt sick and threw the can away. As I was walking back, I saw Christian talking to

---

[112] Let's go drink.
[113] What are you doing?
[114] If you don't chug this, I'm going to tell my dad.

his dad. He told him what we had done. He called Frijolito over, and they spoke for a few seconds. Frijolito came up to me and said it was time to go to sleep. I don't know if his dad was too drunk to care or what, but we both walked inside the trailer.

The next morning, I could hear the adults talking, and I didn't know who had fallen asleep or stayed up. I didn't remember anything; I just remember waking up. Frijolito was already up.

"¿Qué hora es?"[115,] I asked.

"Van a ser las 8."[116]

"Wake me up in an hour," I groaned.

"We're going to miss our game."

"I'm too tired to go," I moaned.

"Andale, chingado ¿Pero anoche qué?"[117] It was the first time Frijolito's dad had talked to me directly.

"He's expecting us to go, doesn't he?"

"I've seen him drink all night and go to work the next day," he responded.

The ride over there wasn't any better. I didn't want to play. Not at all, I didn't want to dress up. I just wanted to go to sleep. From the moment the game started to when it ended, it was a disaster. We played horribly. It was no surprise that we lost. Hard to win when two of the players are running around hungover.

The game finished, and I asked if we could go back and take a nap.

"No puedo, le prometí a mi apa que iba ir a trabajar con el anoche."[118]

I realized that was his punishment.

Instead, they dropped me off at home. My mom was sitting there in the living room.

---

[115] What time is it?
[116] It's going to be 8.
[117] It's time to get, last night you had no issues with that.
[118] I can't, I promised my dad I would go work with him last night.

"Buenos días ¿Como te fue?"[119]

"Buenos días, mom. Bien," I said, heading to my room to nap. I fell asleep thinking about Frijolito. I couldn't believe he was working right now. I felt guilty. I should have been out there working with him too.

---

[119] Good morning. How did it go?

Feliz Navidad

The weather started getting cooler, and the morning air began to hurt my chest when I took breaths in. Winter break was upon us. I pondered about what I was going to do for the next two weeks.

Frijolito had asked me if I wanted to spend Christmas with his family this year. I told him I would let him know since sometimes my mom would have to work early on Christmas, and we would have an early celebration, just the two of us. I figured she would be okay with it as long as I gave her notice.

That afternoon when I got home, my mom informed me that we were spending Christmas in Mexico this year.

That sounded like a great idea. I was a little sad for Frijolito but excited for myself.

The next day I broke the news to Frijolito, and he was thrilled for me. He told me I would enjoy it and to eat as much food as possible.

Christmas had never been a big celebration for me. I never had a Santa come to our house, never took pictures at the mall, or had a chimney. I knew where my mom hid my gifts. I never confessed that to her, but I always knew.

I loved how excited she would get when she woke me up so I could unwrap gifts from Santa.

Once school was over, we headed out. We were going to spend Christmas in Mexico with the rest of my family. I asked her about the gifts she had gotten me, and she explained that it would be best to open them once we got back. I didn't fully understand why, but I didn't argue with her.

After a long and exhausting trip filled with desert, small towns, mountains, and familiar sights, we made it.

I stepped out of the vehicle and faced my grandma's house. As I was crossing the street, I heard a quiet hissing sound. I didn't recognize the sound, but it was followed by a loud bang. It sounded like a gunshot, and my ears began to ring. I was frightened for a second, but I saw a shadow of my cousins disappear. I heard laughter following them.

"Son cohetes,"[120] said my mom as she handed me a bag with groceries to take inside.

I walked inside, and there were family members gathered around the kitchen. Christmas was still a couple of days away, but the celebrations had already begun.

My uncles were off of work and had started drinking.

Outside, it was cold, so my uncles were burning logs while the women were inside cooking and preparing for Christmas.

I don't recall much from that day. I just remember eating and going to sleep.

The following morning, I woke up, the radio was playing, and I could hear stories of Jesus and his birth. The man talking was serious. I just recall my grandma looking at me and saying, "Pon atención."[121]

I just sat in the kitchen waiting for breakfast as the story continued.

I kept zoning in and out of what was happening. In the end, my grandma looked at me and said, "Viste de eso se trata la Navidad."[122]

I just agreed with her.

Nobody was there that morning. Not even my mom. I asked my grandma where everybody had gone. She told me they were getting ready for "La Nochebuena."

"Qué es eso?" I asked her.

It was the 24th. Apparently, Mexicans had their big celebration on the 24th and not the 25th.

---

[120] Fireworks
[121] Pay attention.
[122] This is the true meaning of Christmas.

My mom came in as my grandma was cutting up ingredients for the menudo. I asked her if I could have money for cohetes,

"No son muy peligrosos,"[123] she said.

Then I looked outside and saw cousins half my age playing with fireworks. She didn't change her mind.

I wonder if they were too dangerous for me or if she assumed I was too dumb to have them.

At around noon, my mom took me out of the house. She wanted me to go say hi to some distant family members.

We spent about an hour there, which was awkward for me. I didn't know these people. I had never really interacted with them; if I had, I was too young to remember.

When we got back home, my mom told me to get ready. I told her I was hungry, but she said to me that we had to go to church first, and then we could eat. I didn't want to wait to eat, I was famished.

My mom didn't want me to spoil my dinner, so she told me I would have to wait.

I had never gone to church on the 24th before. I had to put on fancier clothes than usual, and my mom warned me about getting dirty. I didn't like that I had to dress up to church, or that it felt so forced.

I listened and after I showered I sat on the sofa while everybody else got ready. After an hour of sitting there, it was time to leave. That is when I realized that none of my cousins were going. It was just my mom, my grandma, and me. Everybody else had the liberty to opt-out. I didn't.

They all had to get ready for the party later tonight. I wondered what they had been doing all day.

That mass felt eternal. I was hungrier than I had ever been before, I was tired of standing and sitting. The benches were made of old, hard wood. They weren't even comfortable. It just seemed to drag on. I could feel myself starting to fidget on my seat. I knew this would annoy my

---

[123] No, they're too dangerous.

mom, but I couldn't help it. She just gave me a side-eye, so I tried to contain myself as much as possible.

I didn't understand the point of going to church, it wasn't even Sunday. Also, my mom never went to church, so I guess this must have been something special. After a mass that lasted a lifetime, it was time to go home. We had walked here, so I knew that we would have to walk back home.

La Nochebuena

When we returned to my grandma's house, it was already packed. My uncles and aunts wore thick winter sweaters, pants, and boots. All I had were my sneakers. I felt underdressed.

All my cousins were running around looking for something to blow up. I saw one of them grab a glass bottle.

"Las botellas de vidrio no,"[124] I heard on of my uncles yell. I guess almost anything was allowed out here.

The air was cold, but everybody was around the fire.

The sun was already down, and I looked at the clock. Only a few more hours until midnight.

"Aquí viene la quinceañera,"[125] said one of my cousins.

I just smiled at him. I wanted to punch him in the mouth, but I was too hungry to care.

I walked to the kitchen.

There was menudo, buñuelos, pan, tamales, pan dulce, champurrado, birria, and even nopales. I still didn't understand how that had made it on the menu.

When I was allowed to eat, I learned that you had to fight for a seat at the table. People were all waiting to eat, and somebody else would take your seat the moment you got up. Getting up for seconds was risky, even if you weren't done eating.

Everybody was laughing and talking with their mouths full. There was no food etiquette here. I tried to sit down, but an uncle walked in and claimed the chair. He just pushed me to the side and sat down. My mom had gotten me a plate, and he just took it.

---

[124] Not the glass bottles.
[125] Here comes the Quinceañera.

I looked at my mom, who told me to shrug it off, but I couldn't. I was mad, but I couldn't say anything.

After playing musical chairs for dinner, I was finally allowed to eat. Once I had a full stomach, I wanted to stay inside, near the stove, to feel the warmth. I quickly realized that I was surrounded by women and that all the men were outside. I didn't want to be ridiculed, so I went outside with the other men.

I approached the crowd around the fire. Even though there wasn't any snow, it was still cold, and I could feel myself shaking.

All my uncles were just standing around drinking beer and passing a bottle. Everybody would drink from it and pass it down. They handed the bottle to me, expecting me to take a sip. I contemplated it, but I heard my mom yell, "Pobre de ti."[126]

I decided it would be best to pass the bottle down.

My uncles laughed and continued their stories about working construction or how it was going in the mines.

I just stood there in the cold while they were drinking and talking.

Then it got quiet like they ran out of things to talk about. Then one of them turned to me and asked me if I was ready to join the military.

"¿Ejercito?"[127], I asked.

"Si todos los Gabachos tienen que entrar al ejército cuando cumplen 18."[128]

I was confused. This was all new information for me. I didn't know I had to join the military at 18.

"A lo mejor te mandan para Irak"

I didn't know where that was, and I didn't want to go there.

My oldest uncle, Ramon, told us it was time to go inside. I looked at the clock on the wall; it was almost midnight.

---

[126] Don't even think about it.
[127] Military
[128] Yeah you get drafted into the military.

Then about a minute before midnight is when it all began. There were so many bangs going off.

"Cuidado que no todos son cohetes"[129] I heard.

I wondered what that meant. What else could they be besides fireworks?

We weren't allowed to go outside until it finished. I looked at my mom, and she told me, "Son balazos."[130]

Why people would shoot up in the sky is beyond me, but that's how people celebrated here.

I couldn't tell the difference between fireworks and gunshots.

Then once the clock said midnight, everybody went around the room celebrating and hugging each other. Saying "Feliz Navidad" to each other.

Then the presents came out, and all the children opened their gifts. It was mostly bikes, and then my mom pulled out a box filled with gifts from the dollar store. Little cheap toys that my cousins went crazy over. Like they had never received a toy before. It was pure happiness. My mom had instantly turned into Ms. Clause, and she had enough for everybody.

Then people started asking me what I got for Christmas. I didn't know what to say.

"Es que Santa Clause le dejo su regalo en la casa."[131], responded my mom.

I realized two things right there. One, I was more spoiled than the rest of my family in Mexico; two, I was the oldest kid who still openly believed in Santa.

I just nodded my head.

After that, everything was over. Everybody left, and it was over.

The following day, we all cleaned up. It was a strange feeling. As quickly as Christmas had come, it was gone. I was given a shovel and had to clean up the mess from the

---

[129] Be careful because they're not all fireworks.

[130] They're gunshots.

[131] Santa Claus left his gift at home.

night before. All the firework wrappers, beer cans, and other trash had to be picked up. My grandparents didn't even have Christmas lights, so a couple of hours later, Christmas was completely gone.

We left the following day. My mom had to go to work, so we would be spending New Year's in the United States.

Overall, I enjoyed this experience. I learned how Christmas should be celebrated. Or at least how my Mexican family did.

Heads Up

The next couple of weeks passed right on. Nothing exciting or crazy happened. That was until Paulino Mendoza got in my face.

I don't know why, but he just kept trying to aggravate me. Paulino decided to get in my face during class. This made no sense, he was shorter than me, weighed about 20 pounds less than me, and I had never talked to him. Well, not directly, at least. We only had one class together. I figured he just wanted to prove a point.

I was certain that he was going to fight me. He kept asking me, "Let's go, heads up." He asked me during recess when I was in the bathroom, and he would even wait for me after school.

Eventually, Frijolito told me I would have to do something about it.

"I know, but I don't want to fight him."

"You have to if he keeps disrespecting you."

"Disrespecting me?"

"Yeah."

I didn't understand how he was disrespecting me. I just knew I had to do something.

After I had enough of it, I searched for Paulino. I looked for him during lunch, but I couldn't find him. I didn't know where he was.

Maybe he was absent, I thought.

I turned the corner at the end of the hallway and saw him talking to his friends.

I was prepared to approach him and make peace. I was nervous. I could feel my legs shaking. I felt something stuck in my throat. Paulino had his back turned toward me, I wanted his attention, but before I could, he mentioned Sofia.

Frijolito's sister. I couldn't even look at her and here he was talking about her.

I didn't like that. I didn't want to know what he had said about her. I tapped his shoulder, and as soon as he turned around, I just sucker-punched him. I got him right in the mouth, it hurt like hell, and he fell to the ground.

All his friends looked at me and were about to jump me. One of them yelled some things about my mom. Even though he had never met her.

Before anything else happened, a hall monitor grabbed me by the shoulder and escorted me toward the office. I couldn't help but grin as I was being taken away. I had punched Paulino.

As I was being walked, I saw Frijolito, and he made eye contact with me. It had been a while since I had gotten in trouble. I just winked at him.

I waited inside the office for my mom to get there. She had to call off work, which made her furious.

They gave her the short version of what had happened. I punched a kid and instigated a fight.

It resulted in a 3-day suspension.

The principal finished talking, so my mom turned towards me and said, "No television, no video games, no going outside, no going to your game this weekend." She could tell none of this fazed me, "And no Frijolito," she finished.

The last one made me tremor with rage.

I was angry, I felt like crying, but I didn't want to cry. Mexicans don't cry.

The principal spoke up, "It's against the law to not feed your child as punishment, ma'am."

I had never laughed while tears ran down my face before.

I wanted to explain what had happened, but it seemed more important to get out of his office, trying to contain my laughter.

On the drive home, I told her the full version. How Paulino kept bothering me.

She interrupted me, "Who is Paulino?"

"Mom, some kid at school, well, he kept trying to fight me for days, but I kept ignoring it. I kept trying to avoid him, but then he mentioned you and said something disrespectful, so I had to."

Even though she was mad, I guess she understood. "Okay, you're still grounded," she said.

I'm pretty sure she wouldn't have approved if I had told her the truth.

I didn't see Frijolito that week, and whenever he came around, my mom would just remind him that I was grounded.

El Diablo at Church

That Sunday, my mom let me attend church. Since, technically, it wasn't part of the punishment, she knew that I wanted to see Frijolito.

This was the first time that I was excited about going to church.

I even arrived early and waited for Frijolito.

When he got there, I dabbed him up, and we heard the church bells ring, so we took our seats. Mass had started, so we whispered.

"Shhh," we heard behind us.

"¿Entonces qué pasó?"[132], he asked quietly.

I didn't know what to say. I couldn't tell him I wanted to make peace with Paulino. Instead, I lied, I told him I punched him, and that he mentioned his sister Sofia and my mom.

"¿Hablo de mi hermana?", he said, "¿Y de tu mama?"[133], in a louder voice.

I nodded my head.

He was livid. I had never seen him this mad before.

"Shhh," said the lady behind us.

"Usted Shhh!" said Frijolito angrily.

The whole church went quiet. Everybody had heard it.

We looked up, and everybody's eyes were on us. Even the priest paused. I didn't know what to do. We just sat in silence for the rest of mass. When mass was over, the priest waited for us outside. He greeted us and said he would like to talk to us in his office. He made us call our parents. This was different than having your principal talk to your parents.

---

[132] So, what happened?
[133] He talked about my sister? And your mom?

This was your parents and your priest. I knew that day I was going to hell.

When we were all in his office, the priest asked us who had silenced the lady.

I didn't want to snitch on Frijolito, but he eventually confessed that it was him.

The priest looked at him and informed Frijolito that he would have to sit in the front row during the next mass and be an altar boy.

I volunteered myself too. I couldn't have him do that by himself. Both our parents scolded us on the way out. They both kept talking about how embarrassed they were that this was God's home, you know the usual.

All week long, my mom kept reminding me that I would have to be an altar boy.

That following Sunday morning, she dropped me off early at church. Frijolito was already there.

The priest told us that we were forbidden from talking and went over his expectations.

"Esta es la casa de dios,"[134] he said.

We had to wear some robes and wash our hands. We were given the job of carrying the wine and wafers.

I had never had either, but Frijolito had. He could never accurately describe what they tasted like.

Once mass started, the priest walked down the aisle, and we followed him. I could feel everybody's eyes on me, and I saw the lady who had shushed us. Then I got a whiff of something. I noticed that somebody behind us was carrying incense and sage.

Whoever that was placed the thurible next to me.

Mass was different from this perspective. It seemed like all eyes were on us.

We just stood there while everybody sat down, prayed, and sang.

---

[134] This is God's home.

Church seemed to start dragging on. I started to feel nauseous as the smoke blew in my face.

I began getting dizzy.

I couldn't take the sage anymore. I started gagging. I couldn't control it, then I felt my cheeks fill up. I could taste the bile and stomach acid in my mouth. I tried to swallow it back down, but it all came out. Some of it followed through my nose.

I looked up, and even Frijolito was shocked.

I didn't know what to do. Embarrassed, I ran to the front office and called my mom. She rushed to pick me up, and I waited for her. The robe had vomit stains, so I told her what had happened.

"Se te salió el diablo,"[135] she joked around.

It wasn't funny. By the time I returned, I saw Frijolito cleaning up where I had thrown up. That made me feel guilty. It seemed like he was constantly cleaning up after me.

"¿Estás bien?"[136] he asked.

I nodded.

"Se te salió el diablo," he joked.

It was funnier the second time, and I helped him clean up.

As I was scrubbing, I wondered, *Why do Mexicans always joke about things they are superstitious about?*

---

[135] The devil came out of your body.
[136] You good?

Residente o Ciudadana

On the last day before spring break, we had some high school advisors come to school and talk to the students. They mentioned what programs the high schools offered and how to apply. They left us some pamphlets, and most students, including myself, threw them away. Except for Frijolito he kept his and was studying it like if we were going to have a test on it next period.

Once the last bell rang, we would have a whole week off. I was excited about not having school, but then Frijolito told me he would be working that week and didn't think he could come around until the weekend before school started. I was pretty bummed about it, but I understood. We dabbed each other up and walked our separate ways.

I walked by myself, and when I got home, my mother asked me where Frijolito was. I explained that he had to work, and she seemed pretty down about it.

My mom always had the television on and watched the evening news. There was a breaking news alert.

"Mira,"[137] said my mom. She always wanted me to watch the news and see how much others struggled. I don't know if she wanted me to pity them or realize how blessed I was. Either way, it is always sad to see kids without family support or with some type of disability trying to support themselves.

"Pobrecitos," she would say as the segment ended.

Except this time was different. There was a new legislative order.

All I kept hearing was that there was a lot of "Anti-Mexican rhetoric," I didn't quite understand what that meant.

---

[137] Look.

Turns out that a law had been passed that allowed local law enforcement to work with I.C.E. to set up checkpoints throughout the city and question people about their immigration status. People in other states feared it would catch on and become a national phenomenon. It was a massive movement to gather undocumented people and get them out of the country.

This country was built by immigrants and was created by them too. Why didn't that want us here anymore? I wondered.

I looked over at my mom in hopes that she would explain. She just looked at me. She knew I was scared but didn't know how to explain what implications it would have. She tried her best to explain but began weeping uncontrollably. I had not seen my mother cry often. She was the strongest person I knew, but she never shielded her emotions. She encouraged me to share my feelings, even though it was difficult.

"They can't do that?" I asked, "Can they?"

She told me I had nothing to worry about. After all, I was a citizen. But that didn't answer my question.

"You'll be safe too, Mom," I assured her.

"Tal vez, but we don't have the same rights."

I didn't understand what that meant. I thought we were both the same. Before I could ask anything, she searched through her documents for a phone card.

"Just to be safe, I'm going to set up an appointment to get you a passport card."

I had my passport book, but this one was for me to carry at all times. I began to think about Frijolito. I wondered how he was feeling about all of this.

The following Monday, we went into an immigration office, and the line was huge. I had never seen so many people in line for anything before. Not even when I got my passport book, I guess a lot of people were scared of what was happening.

On the ride back home, my mom gave me a piece of paper with all my personal information. My mom folded it perfectly and slid the paper into a wallet she had gotten me.

"You take this and have it on you at all times," I had never seen her this serious before.

"¿Entendido?"[138], she asked me rhetorically.

I asked her why she didn't get a passport for herself and why she mentioned that she didn't have the same rights as me. She pulled out a green card. It was still inside the paper sleeve it came in.

"Soy residente."[139] she said.

I didn't understand the difference between a citizen and a resident. My mom paused and looked at me.

Maybe it was time for me to know the truth about how she ended up in the United States.

---

[138] Do you understand?

[139] I am a resident.

El Amor Falso

My mom and I were sitting at the kitchen table. She took a big sigh and began to tell me about how she ended up in the United States of America.

Before I was born, my mom had met somebody.

There was a guy that would visit Campo Dulce. At first, she never paid any attention to him. He seemed too full of himself and wasn't funny, but he was somewhat handsome, according to my mom. I had never heard my mom talk about checking out another person before, but I guess this was acceptable.

"What was his name?" I asked. She ignored me and continued with the story.

"Anyway, one time we ran into each other, it seemed like an accident. He later confessed that he had been planning to run into her."

"Like a stalker?" I interjected.

She nodded.

Damn, you answered this question but not what I asked you earlier? I thought to myself.

So, he asked her on a date, and she was "young and stupid," my mom's words, not mine. So, she agreed, and they went out to eat.

Then they started to see each other often and began dating shortly after. He would cross the border to Mexico every other weekend just to see her. My grandma told my mom to stay away from him and that he was only trouble, but she didn't listen.

He promised that he would one day take her across the border and that they would live up there. He gave my mom illusions of a better life.

My mom took a break from her story.

"And then what happened? Also, what was his name?"

She looked at me with tears in her eyes. I could tell that this was painful for her to relive. But she continued with her story.

"I fell in love with him. I never thought I would, and after a couple of months, I got pregnant. He was going to be a father, and I was going to be your mother." she said.

Once my mother found out she was pregnant, she waited anxiously for the weekend to come so she could tell him. My mom didn't tell anybody, not her friends or sisters, especially not my grandma. When she saw him that weekend, she was hopeful.

However, when she told him, he didn't seem happy. If anything, he sounded disappointed. And asked her what she was thinking about doing.

My mom just shrugged and said that they would figure it out.

Once that weekend was over, he stopped coming over anymore. She was embarrassed and ashamed. She didn't know what to do. She reached out, hoping he would respond, but he simply said he was busy with work. She never heard from him again, but my mom wanted me to have a better life, so she made plans to travel north to the United States.

She confessed to my grandma what had happened, and they both cried. My uncles and grandpa were furious about this, so they reached out to see if they could find out anything about him.

"Mom, what's his name?"

My mom ignored me and told me they found an address where he lived. My mom said she had an aunt that lived up north. I don't know her actual name, but I know that we called her "Tía Nena."

I don't know exactly how she was related. I think she has my mom's, father's, cousin's, aunt, or something like that. My mom's family had reached out to ask if she could go visit her.

The only problem was that my mom didn't have much money, nor had she done any actual paperwork to come to the United States. My mom decided to use her close friend Nicole's passport. She was desperate and pregnant but determined.

She didn't have much, so she packed a backpack. She didn't have many clothes but figured she wouldn't need much. After a heartbreaking announcement, she left.

She was worried, but there was no turning back. She got on a bus in Hermosillo and headed up north.

When she got to the border checkpoint, Immigration and Customs detained her for questions. She memorized every detail in that passport, but border patrol agents were not satisfied; they had their doubts. The picture of the person did not totally match my mother's appearance. They were convinced it was a different person altogether and denied her entry.

They took the passport away and sent her back home.

My mom mentioned wanting to cry but had no time for that. She decided it was easier to just jump across the border. So that's what she did.

She spotted an opening in the fence and waited. She was certain she would have a better chance if she waited for somebody else to go through so she wouldn't be the only one. Luckily, a group of people planned to cross, so she ran towards them and blended in. When she got through the border, they were spotted by border patrol agents, so everybody rushed through and scattered in different directions. My mom said she ran into a store and pretended to be a shopper. She just saw border agents running past her. She hid in there until she felt it was safe to come out.

She left the store and searched for a phone to call her aunt. She told them she would wait for them in a nearby McDonald's. She waited for hours until her aunt arrived with her husband. My mom was starving, so they ordered food before they drove away.

Once in the car, she fell asleep. When she woke up, they were in the city. My mom gave her aunt an address, and they drove there. They dropped her off and told her to take as much time as needed. My mom wasn't aware of it, but my grandma had reached out to her and informed her of what was going on.

My mom was nervous. She was outside my dad's house. She wanted to go in but didn't know what to say.

She approached the door, but before she knocked, she looked in through the window. There he was at the dinner table, kids were running around, and a woman was sitting at the edge of the table.

He had a family, a wife, two sons, and a daughter. My mom was devastated. He noticed her outside and ran towards her, but my mom had no interest in talking or having anything to do with him.

After that, he tried to reach out to her, but she ignored him. Then after a couple of months, he completely stopped and just forgot about her.

My mom did what she had to, and after I was born, she made sure to get her paperwork in order. Before leaving, she applied for a visa but was denied. Luckily her job helped her get her residency.

When I asked her why she never applied for citizenship, she said, "Look, I tried to cross the border illegally and got caught; I don't know if they have that on record. So, if I try to become a citizen and I lie about it, and that comes up, I will get in trouble. But if I bring that up and they don't have any record of it, I'll get myself in trouble. ¿Entiendes?"

I understood, but there was still one more question I had. "Mom, what was his name?"

"Ah, como chingas[140] Xavier, Oscar, Oscar Zepeda."

"Oscar Zepeda," I said to myself. That's when I learned I had a dad, wherever he was.

---

[140] To bother or annoy somebody.

El Pasaporte

I had a dad, well, kinda, and I also had siblings. Step-siblings? Or half-siblings? It didn't matter; I had a family out there.

I was more upset at my mother for hiding him from me, but I understood that maybe she protected me. He did end up quitting after all. What kind of father would do that?

That weekend I saw Frijolito. It felt like I had not seen him in a while. He told me that he wasn't going to our game that weekend out of fear that there would be police officers there. He told me about the roadblocks all over the city where they had stopped cars and asked people for proof that they were allowed to be in this country.

He wasn't okay. I could hear the fear in his voice.

"Yo tampoco voy a ir al juego,"[141] I told him.

It wasn't much, but I was fine with not going to our game and staying behind. This was the only way I could show him my support.

My mom had to work, so it was just us two. He took out an old, wrinkled pamphlet. I looked at him; it was the one they had given us at school. He seemed pretty excited to share the news.

"Did you know they have a music program?" he asked.

"Who?" I responded.

"Challenger High School", he responded.

He told me he was thinking about applying to the music program.

"Why don't you fill it out then?", I said.

So we both sat there as he filled out the paperwork. He checked off the instruments he wanted to play and began thinking about his future dreams.

---

[141] I'm not going to our game either.

Piano check. Guitar check.

"What about the drums?" I asked him.

"Well, I've always wanted to play in a group, I heard that Mariachis play at Disney World. I could do that, that would be cool. Well, maybe not a Mariachi, but I know they hire a ton of musicians to play."

I realized that we had never shared our future dreams.

That Saturday, I was determined to make sure he turned his application into the high school's admission bin.

Then he turned to me and asked me what I wanted to do when I grew up.

I thought about it, I always wanted to be a professional soccer player, but that sounded dumb.

"A scientist," I said.

"Nice, they also have a robotics program, and a computer program." he said.

I just looked at him and pretended like I was interested.

After he finished the paperwork, I went to my room and got some spare change.

"Where are we going?" he asked.

"To turn in your application," I responded.

"Really?" he asked.

"I really want you to get into that program," I said.

I could tell he was scared about being out in public, especially with everything happening.

"Si nuestros padres se arriesgaron para venir a este país, nosotros le debemos lo mismo si queremos cumplir nuestros sueños,"[142] I told him, and that was all he needed.

I went into my mom's drawer, where she kept all the important paperwork. Inside I found my passport booklet. I returned to the kitchen, where Frijolito was finishing up his application.

Once he finished, I gave him my paper passport. Many numbers and letters had faded, so I wore the picture a little more with a quarter. The picture itself was low-quality,

---

[142] If our parents risked everything to come to this country. We owe them the same if we want to fulfill our dreams.

making it more difficult to confirm who the person on the passport was. It was just a precaution in case we got stopped.

We went outside and walked towards the bus stop. It would just take one ride west, and we would be at the school and another bus east, and we would be back home.

We saw the bus approaching as soon as we got there, but we were on the opposite side of the road. Scared of missing it, I grabbed Frijolito, and we started running. I didn't even check if cars were coming. I was just being reckless.

We made eye contact with the bus driver, who did not look too happy. We were about to get on the bus when I saw a police officer flash their lights.

The bus stopped but then kept going. The driver left us there, abandoned. The police officer got out of his vehicle and started walking towards us.

I had so many thoughts running through my head, *Should I run away from my house and have Frijolito run towards mine and hope I get chased while he keeps running toward my house, or should we pretend like we just got off and calmly walk home?*

I did too much thinking that by the time I finished my thoughts, the police officer was already standing in front of us. I knew I was scared, but Frijolito was visibly shaking. He was more frightened than me.

"Where are you two going in such a rush?"

"To Challenger High School," I responded.

"On a Saturday?" he questioned.

"Yeah," I said as I took the application from Frijolito, "We're going to turn in our application."

The police officer took the packet and inspected it. It had the school logo. It all seemed to be in order.

"The reason I stopped you is because you were both jaywalking. It's not safe to cross the street when there's incoming traffic. Do any of you have identification?"

We both looked at each other. I shook my head, and Frijolito took out the crumpled-up paper.

He looked at the paperwork and wrote down the information, "This is just a warning," he said.

Once he had the information, he hopped into his cruiser and typed it into his computer.

He returned, said that Frijolito was cleared, and asked me again if I had identification; otherwise, he would have to take me to the police precinct. I shook my head once more. I hoped that if I did get taken away that Frijolito would be able to stay, and he could run back home.

Instead, the police officer asked me if I was a citizen. I nodded.

"Great. In that case, let me give you both a ride to the high school," he said.

Frijolito stayed quiet, avoiding eye contact. I said, "No, my mom said I shouldn't get in strangers' cars."

"I'm not a stranger," he assured us.

"Yeah, you're much worse," said Frijolito.

The police officer looked at us. We heard a bus approaching.

We started distancing ourselves from him. Even though we had not done anything wrong, it didn't seem like we were free to go. His radio went off, "We have a 10-12 in progress. We need all available units."

"Copy that," he said into his shoulder and left.

The bus stopped and opened its doors, it wasn't the route we needed, but it was close enough.

We didn't talk during the bus ride. I was relieved, I knew that it was over. At least for me, but this would just be the beginning for Frijolito. We both were afraid, but our fears were not the same.

El Elotero

We got off the bus before it had to turn. It was less than a mile, so it was a walkable distance. While we were walking, I felt exposed. Like somebody could approach us and question us. We were a block away from the school when we heard a bus pass us.

"We should have waited." joked Frijolito.

It was nice to hear him joke again.

We continued walking until we reached the high school. There was a gate around the school.

"We might have to jump this," I told him.

"Nothing new for me," he responded.

I tried not to laugh, but I gave him a smirk.

Once we got closer, we saw a drop-off box next to the gate. A small opening was on it, barely big enough for an application to fit in. Frijolito put the envelope inside and let it go. We heard it slide and drop.

"Es todo," he said.

I felt accomplished and noticed the bus approaching us.

I wanted to motion the bus driver to stop, but we heard a familiar horn.

"El elotero,"[143] I said.

We only had enough money to take the bus, but Frijolito had other plans.

"What if we buy an elote and eat it as we walk home?"

I wondered two things, *One if I wanted a mango instead, but I hated those mango hairs that would get stuck in my teeth. And two, if this was the best idea for us.*

I got nervous and said, "What if we get stopped again?"

"No quiero vivir con miedo,"[144] he said.

---

[143] A man that sells corn on a cob or in a cup.
[144] I don't want to live in fear.

107

I admired that about him.

I would never have to know what living in fear would be like, and if I did, Frijolito taught me that fear was a choice.

A few hours later filled with walking and sightseeing, we made it home. We felt like explorers.

When we got home, my mother was already there.

"Donde andaban vagos?"[145]

We told her we went to the high school to submit our applications. We didn't mention the police officer or the walk. She didn't entirely approve, but there wasn't anything she could do.

"Lávensen las manos pues, vamos a comer."[146]

"Ya comimos," I said.

"¿Qué comieron?"

"Elotes," I said as we went to my room.

We were both exhausted and sore. As we lay there, there was something I wanted to tell him. I just didn't know how to say it. So, I just went for it, "I have a dad"

Frijolito turned to me, "¿Un papá? ¿Y quién es? ¿Te vino a visitar?"

"No," I shook my head, "My mom told me about him."

"Y ¿cómo es?"

I just shrugged.

"Aver dime." He said, trying to get information from me, "I won't tell anybody."

We had never had a conversation like this before, but I told him everything I knew. I shared why my mom came to the United States. How she was searching for him and what she found.

"Eso debe haber sido difícil,"[147] he said.

"¿Fue difícil para ti?"[148,] I asked him.

He just nodded.

---

[145] Where were you?
[146] Go wash your hands and come eat.
[147] That must have been difficult for her.
[148] Was it difficult for you?

That night Frijolito shared his journey across the border. He mentioned his struggles and his most vulnerable secrets. But that night and that story belong to just the two of us.

Promotion

It was the time of year when teachers no longer cared, but neither did the students. We were done with standardized testing, so we didn't have much to do.

The last couple of weeks continued until we reached the final day of school.

We already had the movies and snacks the day before.

Today was about getting our diplomas or whatever you call them. I would be one of the first students called. I wouldn't have many people in the auditorium clapping for me, just my mom. Unlike Frijolito, his whole family would be there cheering and clapping when they called his name. We were all dressed up; some students were already crying while others were fixing their ties. I didn't understand why they were crying if we were all going to see each other again next year anyway.

I saw Frijolito smiling from ear to ear.

"Happy to see me?" I asked.

"Siempre," he said as he held a piece of paper up.

"You got your diploma already?"

"Yeah," he said as I snatched the letter.

I read "Accepted" in big, bold letters.

"What is this?"

"I got into the music program," he said.

I couldn't believe it. He would finally be able to play the piano or the guitar.

"I just have to pick one instrument to focus on," he said.

"That sucks."

"Yeah, but I'll have all summer to decide."

I started shaking out of joy.

I wanted to hug him, I wanted to shout, I couldn't help myself.

I got all jittery, so we got on top of a desk.

Noriega

I started jumping from desk to desk. Frijolito followed me, and we started racing; it was a weird way to celebrate. During one of the jumps, I lost my balance and fell. Face first into the floor, but I wasn't even remotely embarrassed. Frijolito helped me up as everybody stared. I went outside to dust myself off. "Huele a lluvia,"[149] said Frijolito. I began to smell, and it did smell like it was about to rain. I heard my name get called, the ceremony had already started. There was a pause. I pushed my way through people. I heard my mom yelling and screaming as soon as I reached the stage. Even though the principal had emphasized holding the applause until the end. Frijolito's family also joined in. They were so loud, but it felt great to be recognized.

When they called Frijolito's name "Luis Ernesto Flores Bravo," I could feel the whole auditorium shake.

It was a memorable last day of middle school.

After the ceremony, I looked for Frijolito, who was surrounded by his family. I invited him to eat with my mom and me, but his family already had plans. It was a bummer since I was leaving for Mexico the following day.

"So, I guess this is it."

"I'll see you soon," he said.

Before I said bye, I asked him if he wanted me to bring him back anything. Frijolito got all excited and started scribbling on a ripped piece of paper.

The list included papitas, dulces, soda Coca, and a bunch of miscellaneous snacks.

"¿Seguro?"[150]

"Claro que sí,"[151] I told him.

"Gracias, te lo agradezco mucho,"[152] he said.

"De nada," I responded.

Before going our separate ways, I high-fived him.

---

[149] It smells like rain.
[150] Are you sure?
[151] Of course.
[152] Thank you, I appreciate this.

111

"Cuando regreses voy a ser todo un Frijol,"[153] he said as we were walking away.

That made me laugh, it was the dumbest thing I had ever heard, but everything he said made me laugh.

"Okay pues, cuando regrese ya no te voy a decir Frijolito,"[154] I said laughing.

"Ya dijiste," said Frijol.

---

[153] When you come back I will no longer be a small bean.
[154] When I come back I won't call you little bean anymore.

The Prickly Pears

I figured that since it would be my last summer before high school. This would be the last time I would be able to go on adventures and enjoy my summer.

However, my family had plans for me that summer, and it wouldn't be one of those adventurous vacations.

On my second day, my grandpa was up early, before the sun broke the horizon, he made his way to the middle of the desert.

He gave me a shovel but no gloves. All I did was dig holes. Once it was finished, I moved on and dug another one.

Day after day, I dug holes until I finished all thirty-three. My hands were always dirty and had gotten rough from calluses.

After the holes, we had to put on barbed wire to fence the property. I had always wondered who would put these fences up as we drove next to them. Now I knew.

A couple of my cousins were also recruited. At the end of the day, we would all be given a couple of pesos. No bills, just coins. Enough to buy ourselves a Coke.

This is how I spent my first two weeks of summer.

After that, I had chores around the house. I had to collect eggs from the chickens and feed them. I was quickly removed from that position after my grandpa asked me to give the chicks a quick bath. I didn't know what I was doing, and those poor chicks drowned. I felt bad.

My grandpa then handed me a hacksaw and a few blades. There were some old rusty cars in the back that no longer ran and were missing parts, and my new job was to saw these cars apart and put the metal scraps in the back of his Nissan Datsun. At the end of the day, he would take the scraps to the recycling center and sell them. Then he would hand me more saw blades and a few pesos.

He would split the rest of the profits between himself and my grandma. She usually bought groceries, and my grandpa would invest his half on trips to "Las Vegas," which was the local bar. I was responsible for picking him up at the end of the night and walking him home. If he was stumbling, then I had to make sure he wouldn't fall.

It never bothered me that I didn't get paid a living wage. Working gave me a purpose. I understood that the money I was earning was feeding everybody. I learned that everybody here was just surviving.

I realized what poverty looked like.

Midway through the summer, my grandpa took me off scrap metal duty and sent me back to the desert. Only this time, I was equipped with a basket and a metal pole.

I was supposed to get prickly pears. I didn't know what they were. I discovered that they were fruits that grew on top of cacti, and when they were bright red, it meant they were ripe.

I didn't know what to expect, so I wore shorts the first day.

After returning with over a hundred spines stabbing my legs, I decided to always wear pants.

But I learned that no matter how much I avoided those thorns, they would always find a way to get me.

Once I was done, my grandpa would pick me up. I would spend hours taking off all the little splinters stuck to my body. That was the real chore. Sometimes I would forget about them, but then my pants would rub against my leg, and I would feel the thorns going deeper into my skin.

The prickly pears were not for sale. My grandpa just gave them all to my grandma.

My grandma loved them and would make them into jams or eat them once she peeled them. She was always delighted to see me arrive with a full bag. She often encouraged me to try them.

I did once, and they tasted watered down like a sugar-free apple. I guess the pain and suffering of collecting them didn't justify the taste.

That summer, I went from digging holes to being a campesino, to working with metal, to being a picker.

I guess that's where Mexicans get their hardworking ethic from. They start working from a young age.

La Ruta

I did have to go to the state capital once, Hermosillo, Sonora.

We mostly stayed in the countryside. By the mountains and the hills. Where all the roads were made of dirt, and people lived without any shopping centers. I didn't want to go to Hermosillo, but my mom had sent some money, and my tía Rosario, who didn't want to go alone, forced me. She promised we would eat somewhere so that pretty much convinced me.

I had driven past Hermosillo through there on our way to my grandparents, but we went through the edge of the city. I had never stopped or explored the city.

We hitched a ride up north since nobody had a car to take us. Once we arrived, we had to take a local public buses to help us navigate the city.

Hermosillo was crowded and hot. It reminded me of Phoenix. There were so many smells, some good and others terrible, but they all meshed together. The cars were outdated, and there were taxis everywhere. I figured we would take a taxi to the bank. Nope, I was wrong. We had to take a small bus or "La Ruta" as my tía called it.

We waited at this bus stop. Well, it wasn't a bus stop, but just a group of people waiting. There wasn't a sign that said it was a bus stop, and I wondered if people had just started standing there and it had just become an unofficial stop.

We waited, and it wasn't long before a bus came through, and we got on. Not everybody that was waiting got on.

Just a few of us. We didn't say where we were going or anything. I didn't like this bus ride. It didn't have a movie playing. It was hot, the seats were old, and I could feel every bump on the road.

The entrance was in the front, and people exited through the back door.

We walked to the front and paid our 5 pesos. Which is equivalent to a quarter.

As we rode, I looked out the window. I didn't know how big the city was, but it seemed massive. I couldn't locate myself. I saw my surroundings, but nothing looked familiar.

I knew I would get lost if I weren't with my aunt, but I didn't feel afraid.

At every street light, there were street performers. Some people juggled balls, and others swallowed knives and tons of pyromaniacs. It felt like I was at a circus.

After a while, we reached our destination. We hopped off the bus and headed out. We were still a couple of blocks away from the bank.

I noticed a store that sold all kinds of knock-off shirts and sweaters. They were so cheap.

I could dress like the cool kids, I thought, *Or I could get a matching shirt for myself and Frijolito.*

We walked into the bank, and inside, a man was holding a rifle and making sure we didn't have any hats or anything that covered our faces.

We waited in line and then walked up to the register. My tía took out my passport. I was confused and conflicted.

Why did she have my passport? Were we close to a border?

I felt uneasy, but I trusted her.

The teller looked at me and put his hand out as she handed him my passport. He reviewed the document and looked at his screen.

After a few moments, he returned my passport and opened a cash drawer.

He put money down on the counter and began counting it. After he finished counting, he handed the stack of bills to my tía and made me sign a slip of paper.

I didn't even have a signature, so I just wrote my name. Nothing special. "Xavier Barrera."

As we were walking out, my tía told me that my mom had sent the money under my name, and that's why I needed to provide my passport.

I thought about it and realized the money was technically mine, but it wasn't for me.

I noticed that my mom had sent extra money, and my tia told me it was for me. I was delighted to know that my mom had sent me an extra 300 pesos, but then she asked me if I could buy her food and realized that the lunch I was promised would be my treat.

I didn't know where to eat, she suggested a restaurant nearby and said we could take "la ruta," once again.

We walked to one of those "bus stops" where people just stood around.

We saw the bus approaching, but before we got on, my aunt gave me the envelope with the money and told me to stuff it inside my shoes. I did, but I was afraid somebody else had noticed.

The bus stopped, and I heard the wheels squeak to a stop. After a second, the doors opened, and we climbed on.

As we were riding downtown, I saw the artwork and different performers. It was exciting.

Suddenly, I felt the bus slowing down. I looked forward and noticed the street light was still green. I didn't see any railroads, so I didn't know why we were stopping. I figured this must have been one of those random unofficial bus stops.

The bus driver came to a complete stop and opened the doors. An individual ran through the entrance while another one blocked the back exit.

I didn't understand what was happening, then I figured out that we were getting robbed.

He was walking down the line telling people to give him their money. While waving a gun around. It reminded me of the church when they would walk down the aisles asking for money with the basket.

I made eye contact with the thief. I don't know if it was accidental or on purpose, but it happened. I could feel myself shaking. I didn't want to be afraid or scared, but I could feel myself trembling and getting tears in my eyes. I knew I wasn't going to die, but I just didn't want to be in that position. I wanted to run away, but I had nowhere to go.

I think he saw how scared I was, skipped a few rows, and made his way towards me. He pointed his gun at me and asked me for everything I had. I only had 300 pesos in my pockets. 100 in one pocket and 200 in the other. I had separated them. The rest of my money was in my shoe.

I looked over at my tía; she had spent the whole time looking out the window. It was like she was used to this. She knew what was happening and already had spare coins out. That was all she had.

He simply put his hand out and wanted me to give him what I had. I gave him 100 pesos from my right pocket. He didn't seem satisfied like he knew I was lying. He put the gun up to my head. It wasn't cold. But it was sticky and slightly wet. Like the paint had not dried off yet.

I looked him in the eyes and pondered for a split second what I should do. I didn't know if the gun was real, but I didn't want to risk it. I started feeling the adrenaline run through my body and I smirked at him.

"Dame todo lo que tienes."[155]

I just looked at him and shrugged.

He wanted more. He asked if I had any phones, jewelry, or more cash. I just shook my head. He knew I was lying. I had a terrible poker face. He knew I had more money stashed away, but he feared that I knew that his gun might have been fake.

He looked at me. I wasn't sure if he wanted to hit me or not. I was being stupid. I was gambling my life away for 200 pesos but had to keep up my lie.

---

[155] Give me everything you have.

I heard a car behind us honk. They both looked up and took off. Just like that, it was all over. I didn't feel courageous. I felt stupid, but I also felt ashamed of being Mexican.

My tía told me to promise not to tell anybody about what had happened. I promised her I wouldn't. She smiled, and I could see she was still shaken up about what had happened, even though she tried to pretend she was calm. I reached into my pocket and gave her what I had left. She smiled.

We had tacos that day and a couple of sodas, they were pretty disappointing. They were delicious, but they weren't to die for.

After that, we went to a bus station where I gave her everything my mom had sent out of my shoe. We got tickets for a bus that would drop us off close to home, one with comfy seats and that played movies.

As we were leaving, I looked out the window. I realized that Mexico wasn't the perfect place I had envisioned.

The murals on the walls looked dull, and the city looked dirty. I didn't feel unsafe, but I began to realize the truth about my beloved country.

I always wanted to be Mexican, but I didn't know if it was something I would be proud of.

El Caldo de Pollo

On the ride back, my tía could tell I was upset. She knew that I was bothered more than I wanted to let on. "Se siente feo, pero es parte de la vida,"[156] she said. I didn't want to recognize this reality of life. I tried to ignore it and continue living in bliss and ignorance. "Una vez también lo hice yo."[157] I looked at her. My tía had always been a saint. Then she started to reminisce about her life. My aunt shared that since they grew up on a ranch, my grandparents would often leave to work in Hermosillo. My aunts and uncles had to stay at the ranch to care for the animals, so they never received proper schooling. That made me sad.

My grandparents would visit periodically with supplies and left my aunt in charge. She was the second oldest in the family but was burdened with caring for all my uncles and aunts. She even took care of her older sister. I don't know what characteristics a person has to be born with to be responsible for older siblings. She was a lot older than my mother, so by the time she had her kids, she still had to watch my mom since her daughter, my cousin Camila and my mom were only a couple of months apart.

Mexican families have siblings, cousins, aunts, and uncles all the same age. Family trees get messy, but you somehow know you're all related.

"Una vez me dejaron cuidando a los chamacos," she continued, "Pero no me dejaron comida. Y no tenía para darles, y no sabía lo que iba hacer. Esa mañana oí el gallo de la vecina y salí hacia afuera y miré que iba de salida. No sé

---

[156] I know it sucks, but it's a part of life.
[157] I had to do that too once.

para dónde iba, pero mire que una de sus gallinas andaba caminando sola por la casa."[158]

I looked at her and thought, *You did not steal that chicken.*

That's exactly what she did, though. She stole the chicken from her neighbor. She stole a chicken...

My aunt set a path of rice that the chicken followed until it was trapped inside the house. When the chicken realized that had happened, it was already too late.

"Y luego qué pasó."

"Nada, a la tarde la vecina regreso y se dio cuenta que le faltaba una gallina. Todos estábamos comiendo en la meza y me pregunto que se había mirado la gallina. Y le dije que no, mientras le servía caldo de pollo a todos."[159]

I couldn't help but laugh. My aunt was a chicken thief and a liar.

I didn't know what the point of the story was, but I started to think about it. Maybe she wanted to tell me that stealing was normal to Mexicans. Or maybe we all had to eat, and it was better to be a thief than to be hungry.

Regardless, I learned my aunt was wild and saw where my mom got it from.

For the rest of the trip, she continued to share stories. It reminded me of Frijolito. She began to explain family trees. About who my distant family members were and how we came to be.

She told me about my mom, about who she was as a child, and she retold my mom's journey. She even talked about my dad. Besides my mom, nobody had mentioned him

---

[158] One time your grandparents left me the kids, but they didn't leave me any food. I didn't have anything to give them. I didn't know what to do. Then I heard the neighbor's rooster and saw that she was leaving. So that meant that the chickens were alone.

[159] Nothing, when she came home later that day she asked me if I had seen her chicken and I said no. While we were all eating chicken soup.

to me before. It was different. It was the story my mom told me from a different perspective but with the same ending. I couldn't help but feel sad, but then she told me about my childhood. My first years on earth. She told me stories about things I did that I couldn't remember. It was surreal knowing that there were parts of me that I didn't know about.

My mom would send disposable cameras so they could take pictures of me and send them back to her. I asked her why there were so many pictures of me eating dirt. She started laughing.

"A tu mamá no le gustaba verte sucio."[160]

"Entonces?"

"Nomas se las mandábamos para hacerla enojar,"[161] she said laughing.

I couldn't believe it; they would prank my poor mother and make me eat dirt just to send those pictures to my mom. I mean, it's not like she could do anything about it.

I could imagine my mom getting those pictures developed and having a heart attack at the local CVS.

My tía Rosario even shared how much my grandma loved caring for me. She even joked and said it was the first time my grandma had taken care of a baby.

That made me laugh. She told me that leaving me was difficult for my mom. That she missed out on my first steps and my first words. That she wasn't a part of my life during that time. It was sad, but she then reminded me that she made those sacrifices so I could succeed in life.

She continued talking about how I was a travieso [162]and a terco[163]. That I would constantly be climbing cabinets and furniture around the house. No matter how often I fell or hurt myself, I would not stop.

---

[160] Your mom didn't like to see you dirty.
[161] We would just send them to her just to make her mad.
[162] Mischievous
[163] Stubborn

"Pero síguele," they would say to me, and I would take it literally and climb until I fell again.

I started laughing.

Then I heard a voice on the speaker and realized we had made it to our stop.

El Mundial

When we got back home. It seemed like everything was back to normal, and nobody asked us about the trip. My tía didn't say anything, and we arrived just in time for the cafecito. [164]

I could see in her eyes that she didn't feel the need to share what had happened.

I wondered what other stories she had kept to herself or how many hardships she had been through that she chose not to share. She had always been a rugged individual. I guess life had shaped her to be that way.

The rest of the day went smoothly. That was until the soccer game started. This was the game everybody had been talking about for days. Mexico's national team had momentum and showed that they could play with the big teams. Everybody gathered around the television. It wasn't difficult to find the game since there were only two channels.

There were snacks and people all around the living room. It was loud and noisy as everybody talked, and you could feel the excitement in the air.

All my uncles had a beer in hand. As always, there was a cooler outside, filled with just beer.

If any of us were thirsty, all we had was water.

The game started. It was Mexico vs. Holanda. I had never heard of that country. I just knew it was a brand of expensive ice cream.

The game was very close. Mexico had never made it this far before. We had waited four years for this moment.

Everybody in the room was silent. You could feel the tension building up. We were helpless. All we could do was watch.

---

[164] Evening coffee

125

Finally, Mexico scored, and we all went wild. We were yelling and screaming. It was a level of happiness I had never reached before. It was like seeing history unfolding.

The rest of the game continued.

"Cabron,"[165] I heard my tío Armando yell.

Followed by an "Ah pendejo,"[166] from my tío Marcos.

I felt more and more nervous as the minutes counted down.

It seemed that Mexico was bending but not breaking, but then it happened. They got scored on. The game was tied 1-1. It wasn't hopeless, but I could feel reality setting in. Mexico was crumbling.

The once loud room became silent. Then the announcer broke the silence, "Penal, Penal, Ppppeeeeeeeeeennnnnnnnnaaaaaaaaaalllllllllll."

A penalty. It was against Mexico. It was against us.

We all watched the replay. We were all in disbelief, "No era penal," somebody screamed. "No era penal," we all repeated.

The Netherlands' captain lined up. We prayed he'd miss. That was the last hope we had. Sadly, he ended up scoring, and Mexico never recovered. Moments later, we were eliminated. All of our dreams were crushed.

It was the second time that day that I had been robbed.

My uncle got up and turned off the T.V.

We would have to wait another four more years.

Nobody knew what to say, so everybody just slowly left the room.

I went outside. My grandpa made fun of me for being sad. He told me I was American and should have been rooting for the US National team either way.

I just wanted to be left alone. That's all I wanted.

I went outside and cried by myself. I didn't want anybody to see me. I kept repeating, "No era penal," over and over again.

---

[165] Dumbass
[166] Idiot

That was my first heartbreak.

My Summer's End

The rest of my summer was filled with more work, a nice distraction from the wistfulness surrounding me. I began counting down the days until it was time to return home. My mom was actually driving down to pick me up.

I kept a mental calendar. I didn't write it down or tell anybody I was looking forward to leaving. I didn't want them to feel that I didn't appreciate them or wasn't having fun. In reality, I was, but I was feeling homesick.

That was till I finally saw my mom pulling up to the driveway. Seeing her get out of her car was bittersweet. Even though this summer passed by in a flash, I missed her. She was going to stay for a week, but I knew it was getting closer to going back home. Back to see my best friend, and back to school. In the back of my head, I knew I had to get ready for high school.

I was officially going into high school and could not believe it. I was a few days away from being a freshman. I was nervous about starting up in a new place. But also excited, I wondered what adventures Frijolito, and I would go on. I had always heard that being a freshman sucked because upperclassmen picked on you. Still, it sounded better than being a middle schooler.

The day before we had to leave, I got the list of items that Frijolito wanted. I kept it hidden in one of my grandma's Bibles since I knew nobody would go through it. Suddenly I felt somebody behind me, and it was my grandma. She seemed excited over the fact that I was reading the bible. In reality, I was just retrieving my list, but I couldn't hurt her feeling like that. So, I pretended to continue reading. I looked over and saw my mom laughing at the door. She saw the whole thing and looked at the list and smiled.

It wouldn't be an expensive shopping spree, but I knew it would make Frijolito's day. My mom even tagged along and did some shopping of her own. While she did that, I made sure to get everything on the list. I didn't want to forget a single item. We stopped for some tortillas, queso, and even natural honey that came in a glass jar.

I missed Frijolito. He was my best friend, after all. The thought of seeing him put a smile on my face.

Before leaving the next day, we had a last family meal. All my cousins, uncles, aunts, and anybody remotely related came over. We ate and laughed. My mom made sure to take pictures of me with my grandparents and to get one of everybody in the family. We all got quiet and smiled, which was not an accurate representation of who we were since the whole house was loud and chaotic. Looking at them, I found it difficult to understand that everybody in the picture had come from just two people. We sure did multiply and fast.

After a couple of hours of sitting around, eating, and talking, it was finally time for us to leave.

Nobody in the family had gotten their visas renewed, so this trip was just going to consist of my mom and myself. As I was saying goodbye to everybody, my uncles approached me and told me to take care of my mom and keep her safe.

Like bro, I'll try my best, but no promises, I thought, *I mean, I would take care of her the best way I could.*

My mom had my uncles check and ensure everything in the car ran smoothly. First, my uncles checked the tire pressure; well, they did this test where they kicked the tires and then unanimously decided that they were good enough. Then, they checked the oil and antifreeze. Everything was fine, except we were low on gas. We would have to make a stop before heading out.

At the gas station, my mom forced me to go pee. I didn't feel like going, but she knew that if I didn't go, then I would be bugging her down the road.

I had to force myself to pee.

After washing my hands, I walked back to the car.

"¿Measte?" she asked me.

"Yes, mom, I peed."

"Not on yourself?" she said laughing, "Like last time."

"Mom," I groaned.

She couldn't let it go.

See, what happened was that I needed to pee badly. I couldn't hold it, so I begged her to pull off the road and stop. She told me we were almost home and to hold it, but I couldn't.

After continuously nagging her, she stopped on the side of the road, and I ran off and tried to pee by some bushes, but nothing happened. I just couldn't pee. I guess it was the pressure of wanting to pee so desperately. I just stood there, and after 5 minutes of just standing there, I finally gave up. I walked back to the car, defeated. It all came out as soon as I got in the car and buckled my seatbelt. I had no control.

I peed myself and didn't have a logical explanation for why that happened. My mom was too mad to scold me, so she just laughed and told me I had to wash her leather seats.

Even though we were like 10 minutes from our destination, it was the longest ride of my life. I asked her to let me change, but she wasn't having it. She just let me sit there in my peed pants. We were almost home, so it wasn't a punishment, and nobody ever found out besides her. It was a joke between us two, and I appreciated that she didn't embarrass me, but she did make fun of me about it often.

The Gallons of Water

After driving for hours, we were finally near the border. It seemed like there might have been been some kind of accident when we saw how long the line was. It was longer than I had ever seen it. My mom even confessed that she had never seen that many cars before. There was no explanation for why it was so long. There just happened to be a lot of people crossing that weekend.

As we drove, we noticed some cars were overheating while others were running out of gas. That's when I knew we would be here for a while. We had left my grandparents' house early, but it was already closer to dinner time by the time we got to the border. The border was open 24 hours, but still. We did not expect the line to be this long.

The first couple of hours were easy; we spent the remaining money on snacks. We had paletas de arroz, duros, mangos con chile, and anything else we could find. We eventually got tired of snacking. It wasn't like we were hungry. There just wasn't anything else to do.

After that, we just kept turning people down. Mostly saying, "Ahorita no," whenever they would come to sell us little trinkets. They had anything ranging from shot glasses, bracelets with your name, jewelry, bags, blankets, toys, balloons, la lotería, piggy banks, and vases. They had belts that they claimed were made from nopales.

We had to turn them down too. I was surprised I had never heard of that. My mom just looked at me and said, "They'll sell you anything and everything they can here, and if it can't be sold, they'll turn it into something that can be."

I looked up periodically and did mental math to estimate how much longer it would take us. After a while, I saw we were getting closer to the border. This trip was taking longer and longer, and time kept slowing down. After 4 hours of waiting in line, I was mentally done. The sun was barely creeping out, but it was still hot. Even with the A/C on, I was getting warm. Luckily the sun would only be out for another hour or so.

I could finally see the actual border crossing point, it still looked like it was about a kilometer away, but at this point, it would be another hour or two.

My mom looked at her dashboard and realized she was running low on gas. We knew we wouldn't make it. We had to do something.

She suggested I walk to a gas station and buy two water gallons.

"¿De agua?" I interrupted, confused because I was sure our car ran on gas, like most cars.

She then instructed me to throw out the water and fill it with gas.

I was always pleasantly surprised by how people think of solutions like this.

I exited the car and walked a couple of blocks asking vendors for the closest gas station, which was only 3 blocks from where we were.

I walked inside the gas station and saw a line of people. All of them with water jugs. Mostly men, but there were some women and children. They all had backpacks and put their water jugs inside of them.

My mom is smart, but these people are smarter, I thought. They probably all came up with the same solution.

After paying for the water gallons, I walked outside and started to dump the water in the street. Some people looked at me and asked why I was throwing the water out. I explained that I needed the gallon jugs to fill them up with gasoline.

They offered to trade their empty gallons for mine. I was confused; it wasn't a fair trade, but it made sense.

We traded, and they thanked me. I turned to the man in charge of filling the cars with gasoline and asked him to fill the gallon jugs. He looked at me and took the Mexican Pesos bills I had. When he was finished, he instructed me to be careful and to turn the car's engine off before putting it in the tank.

Noriega

I nodded my head and left.

As I walked back, I didn't recognize any cars there. The buildings looked familiar but nothing else. I figured the line had moved more than I had predicted, or maybe I had taken longer than it felt. I started walking north and finally saw my mom's car. I approached her and told her to turn off her car.

She did, and I carefully filled her gas tank to not drop any gasoline on me. With those two gallons, we managed to get almost a quarter of a tank. Not a lot, but enough to get us across the border.

I returned to my seat, and my mom told me I smelled like gasoline. I wanted to share what I had just done and how I traded the gallons when we saw busses stopping on the United States side of the border.

The buses opened their doors, and people started coming out. All surrounded by border patrol agents. There were at least one hundred people, mostly men, crossing back. I noticed they were being escorted by Mexican people in navy-blue uniforms.

As they were walking, they started getting separated into two groups. Some looked exhausted, while others looked defeated. But they all seemed hopeless.

I looked at my mom, who also noticed them.

I asked her what was happening, and she told me with a melancholy tone, "Los deportation."

That's when I learned that those people lived in the United States until recently and were being sent back home. Coming home should always be a happy experience, but coming home like this was the opposite, there was nothing happy about this.

I asked her why they were being separated and who the people in the blue uniforms were.

"Aduana,"[167] she said.

Her response didn't answer my question or explain who they were. She kept looking at them.

---

[167] Customs

133

"Those are the Mexican customs agents, separating them to see where those people need to go. They might all be Mexican, but they're not all from here."

"So, they're like Mexican border patrol?"

"Más o menos."

I looked at them. They were being shepherded by Mexicans in Mexico like they were prisoners.

I saw a couple of them run across the streets and take off. Nobody went after them; I figured that they weren't in trouble.

I wanted to ask why they had run off, but how would she have known.

Then as quickly as they had arrived, they had disappeared. They had all gone their separate ways back to reality.

I looked at the gas tank, and we still had more than enough gas to get through.

We were almost at the border, just a couple of cars ahead of us, when I looked out towards the desert. Where nothing had been built yet, a place filled with bushes, trees, and dirt. On the horizon, the sun was almost done setting. It was getting dark, but there was still enough light to see what was out there.

I noticed silhouettes at a distance in the direction where the men had run off to. It looked like a caterpillar making its way to shelter itself in a tree. Moving slowly but with rhythm. I looked at my mom and pointed them out. You just saw a row of people crossing, making their way towards the border. Hoping to make it over.

They all had backpacks, and I wondered if the person I had exchanged the water jugs with was on that journey.

My mom looked at them and said, "Pobrecitos, y les deseo buena suerte."[168]

I just sat there quietly, *Why not wish luck to the ones who stayed here. Why did they have to leave in the first place?*

---

[168] Poor things, I wish them all luck.

The Border Patrol

Finally, after all this waiting time, we reached the checkpoint. We were next in line.

I was tired from just sitting down and started reflecting. My mom turned off the radio. I already knew the drill. I was not supposed to speak or do much. Just nodded my head when my name was called.

I started thinking about Frijolito and what he had told me in one of our conversations. I tried to understand how difficult crossing the border might have been for him. I mean, he was just a kid, after all.

I realized how lucky I was to be born in this country and how that simple fact alone made my life so much easier. I started feeling grateful but guilty.

I reflected about how I was complaining that I was tired of sitting and getting hungry when people were walking, and all they had was water. Water and hopes that they would make it to a better future.

"Xavier," I hear a deep voice yell out.

I looked up and saw a border patrol agent looking at me and down at my passport.

"Present," I said.

My mom looked at me, and she gave me some type of side-eye.

The agent went back into his little window and typed into his computer.

"Sorry, Mom. I guess I zoned out and started thinking about the people crossing."

"People crossing?" responded the officer back.

I couldn't believe what I had just said. How dumb was I? The correct answer is very. Man, what kind of Mexican sells his own people out? Then I remembered what my mom had said about how Mexicans would sell anything they could. I

135

instantly regretted what I had said. Even the people that deported all those Mexicans gave them a ride on a bus while I'm over here throwing them under one.

I was too ashamed to look at my mom.

The border patrol agent became suspicious and placed my mom's card, my passport, and a piece of paper on the windshield. He directed us to the revision area.

This had never happened to me before.

There were immigration officers all over us. They told us to leave our phones, wallets, keys, and documents in the car.

The agents escorted us to a small, gray room with no windows and made us sit in cold metal chairs. I looked around and saw nothing but cinder blocks, this looked like a prison cell, and there was nothing for us to do there. We heard a loud buzzer, and the gate closed on us.

I sat there quietly and looked at my mom. She just gave me a set of hopeful eyes, nothing more or less. That was fine with me because it was all I needed.

After about 15 minutes, we were called back and returned to our car. We saw that they had gone through everything. The trunk and hood were open, and they had removed one of the front lights, breaking it in the process.

Before leaving, my mom brought it to their attention, and they claimed that they were not responsible for any damages. That irritated my mom and made me feel worse.

We got inside the car, and I apologized to my mom as we drove away. She simply looked at me and winked. I loved it when she did that.

Cloudless Rain

The drive after that went smoothly, but it still took time. When we finally got home, we were exhausted. Completely wiped out and tired.

I wanted to sleep, but my mom told me I had to take the bags in and clean the car before showering and heading to bed. She carried some bags with her and helped me out as much as she could. After a couple of trips going back and forth, I finished. I went inside and saw that my mom had fallen asleep on the couch. She must have been drained.

The next morning, I woke up early and found a piece of paper on the table. There was no sign of her; she had already left to work. It was a list of chores I had to do before leaving the house.

I missed Frijolito and just wanted to run to his house. I was not embarrassed to admit that. I did everything the list told me to do.

I cleaned my room, folded the clothes, washed the dishes, and even took out the trash.

I grabbed the bag with all of Frijolito's stuff and ran outside, I could hear the phone ringing inside, but I figured it was my mom, and she would understand why I didn't answer. The weather was excellent, and not a single cloud in the sky. Just a day filled with sunshine.

I began to walk after a while. I was impatient but excited, but I didn't want to seem too eager. I was filled with pure joy and happiness. I was walking to see my best friend. I had done this before, but this time it was different. I turned the corner into his trailer park.

I walked to the one where he lived. His dad's truck wasn't in the lot. There was just an oil spill in the bottom. I walked up to the entrance, but it was empty. I knocked, but there was no answer. I waited outside for what felt like hours, but it was only a couple of seconds. I looked inside through the window and saw that there wasn't anything inside. No furniture, no television, and no sign of Frijolito. I didn't know what to do or where to go. I just stood there, waiting for somebody to answer the door.

I could feel the tears were starting to build up. I tried to keep them from coming down. I didn't know how to react. I looked at the trailer again and hoped that I was at the wrong one and had made a mistake. That Frijolito would be behind me and laugh at me. I just wanted him to be there, but he wasn't.

I just grabbed the bag and walked back home. I felt defeated. I could feel the drops of water going down my cheeks and into my chin. I didn't want to look up. I wish it was raining so I couldn't feel the tears going down my face, but no amount of rain could shield me from what I was feeling.

Sadly, there was no rain. There wasn't any rain smell, no clouds, nothing.

Just me crying, looking at the sun. I kept everything I had brought him. The candy, soda, and chips. I had the list of everything he missed, and that's all I had left of him.

That was my second heartbreak, I had lost my best friend, and I've been looking for him ever since.

Home Counseling

When I got home. My mom wasn't there, just me. I had never felt so alone, even when I didn't have friends had I felt this alone. I felt like something was missing or forgotten. I was so optimistic and cheerful earlier, but now that feeling was gone. I wondered where Frijolito was. I hoped he would come through the door and ask me how I'd been. I thought that would make me feel better, but he didn't.

My mom got home after work and saw me in the kitchen. I had not moved. She saw the bag of goods and asked me why I still had them.

I explained to her what had happened. That nobody was home. That I cried on the way home, wishing it was rain. She hugged me, and it was a good hug. It was a hug I needed and a hug that nobody else could give me.

"¿Qué le pasó ama?"[169]

"No sé."

"You think he got deported or that they just moved?"

"No sé," she repeated gloomily.

It wasn't like he was dead, but he was gone without a trace. He didn't leave me a note or anything.

The rest of the week felt like it dragged on. I knew I should have been getting ready for school. But I wasn't. I was difficult to get excited about school.

My mom tried her best to cheer me up, and I appreciated that, but there was nothing she could do. I was sad. I think I just needed to mourn the loss of my best friend. He wasn't dead, but I knew that I wouldn't be seeing him.

My mom told me that maybe I would see him in high school if he moved to a different house. Maybe I would run into him.

---

[169] What happened to him, Mom?

I didn't get my hopes up. I just didn't want to be disappointed.

My mom encouraged me to go shopping for back-to-school items. New shoes, a new backpack, and school supplies. I told her I didn't want anything new. I just wanted my old friend.

That was the longest week of my life. Nothing I did brought me any joy. It was just an empty feeling of nothingness.

My mom worried and speculated if maybe I had depression. I didn't. I was just sad, but she wanted me to see a counselor. I didn't want to do that, so I just began to pretend that I was getting better. It was like I was imagining that I was somebody else. I would only pretend when my mom was home. When she wasn't, I would just daydream on the couch.

I would turn on the television, hoping it would drown the silence and have some noise around the house. It helped. I would just think about all the times I had with Frijolito, the dumb laughs, and how he was always there for me.

When my mom got home that weekend, she told me that my coach had called her. There was an emergency meeting. I told her that I didn't want to play anymore, and she told me that she understood that, but maybe they could tell us something about Frijolito.

There were only a handful of parents when we got to the park. We were missing about half of the team; I didn't see Frijolito anywhere. Then our coach told us that the team would dissolve and that we were welcome to merge with one of our rival teams since so many players had been lost. He mentioned that he didn't know specifics about people but that many of my teammates had moved back to Mexico.

Once he was finished, another coach stood up and introduced himself. He welcomed us all and invited us to join his team since he had also lost half of his. He wanted to continue coaching, so he gave us his contact information before we left.

Noriega

On the drive home, I gave the slip of paper to my mom. I told her I didn't feel like playing soccer, at least not in the near future and definitely not right now.

Challenger High School

After a dreadful weekend of absolute sadness, it was Monday morning. I wondered how many people felt like this often. And how they snapped out of it?

When I decided to get up from bed, my mom was already getting my backpack ready. She could sense my sadness and just wanted to make my life easier. I told her she didn't have to, but I did appreciate the kind gesture.

Before leaving, she made me stand by the door and, like at the beginning of every school year, told me to smile. She loved taking pictures of me on the first day of school.

"Sonríe,"[170], she said.

I did my best to fake a smile. I saw the flash, and she just said, "Oh, otra mejor."[171]

We did that for a few minutes, but I was already over it.

She told me to get in the car, and I asked her, "I thought I had to take the bus?"

"You will, but today I'll take you. Plus, you have to be early to get your ID picture."

I liked that. I was pretty nervous. As I walked across the car, I saw the dent we had made when Frijolito and I had driven her car. My mom looked at me and asked me, "¿Quién fue? ¿El Frijolito o tu?"[172]

I pretended like I didn't know what she was talking about.

"¿Qué crees? ¿Qué nací ayer?"[173] she finished.

Why do all moms say that? Obviously, she wasn't born yesterday, I thought to myself.

---

[170] Smile.
[171] Another one.
[172] Who was it? Was it you or Frijolito?
[173] Do you think I was born yesterday.

I didn't answer, I just put on my seat belt, and we drove to the school.

"I know you miss him," she said, "but I'm sure you'll make new friends."

I didn't say anything, but that didn't mean that I didn't want to say something. I wanted to explain that I didn't want to make new friends and missed Frijolito. That I was not ready to replace him. I don't think I would ever be ready. I didn't say any of that. I just nodded my head.

We arrived at the school. There was a route for parent drop-offs, and she told me that I had to take the bus home and gave me some money for the bus. I had already taken the bus to school before, so I knew the route.

The air was surprisingly cold, and I could see clouds beginning to form.

Before getting off, my mom wished me luck and kissed me.

"I love you, Xavier."

"Okay, Mom. I'll see you later," I said and exited the car.

As I was closing the door, she rolled the window down.

"I said I love you, Xavier," she yelled.

You could see the shock on my face. I didn't know what to say, but I figured she was trying to cheer me up by embarrassing me.

I yelled even louder, "I love you too, mom."

I could feel people looking at me, but I didn't care. I was a little embarrassed, but I truly loved my mom.

I looked down at the schedule I received when I enrolled in school.

I felt lost. I didn't know where any of my classes were. I walked around, looking for the assembly hall. I just followed the other lost-looking kids since they were probably freshmen too. They would eventually lead me to where I had to be.

That first day was more than I had anticipated. There were so many people, everybody was busy. People were going in all different directions. Everybody was walking like they were in a rush.

I was experiencing a cultural shock. Once again.

I knew where this was coming from. When I started my schooling, I was a minority. Then I went from a minority to a majority overnight in middle school. However, this was different. This high school was culturally diverse. I could tell that there were more than just Mexicans here. I could hear it in their voice. Their Spanish was not like my Spanish or any that I had heard.

There were Native people, Asian people, and Black people. I saw people wearing Dashikis, something that I had never seen before. They were so colorful and reminded me of Mexican serapes.

I want one of those, I thought to myself.

I also noticed European-American people.

There was such a mixture of cultures. It was like I was in a whole new world. I had never gone to a school with so many differences.

I saw that people were lining up to get their pictures. Like sheep, I just followed them and had mine taken. It was all a fast process, but it came out worse than the 57 pictures my mom had already taken earlier.

There were still a couple of minutes before the bell. I just stood there and looked at what was going on around me.

I began to wonder if this was the right place for me. I knew I wouldn't fit in anywhere because I was so different from everybody around me. I began to panic, but before I could run away, I heard the bell ring, and security started yelling.

"Get to class, don't be late."

I opened the doors to enter the building and began looking for room E202.

When I found my classroom, I walked in and saw that there were already students sitting down. I wasn't the last one in, but I was not comfortable.

I saw an open desk and sat down. Another classmate approached me and introduced himself. He was tall and thin, obviously of European descent. His hair was light, and so were his eyes. They were a shade of light green I had never seen before. He walked in with a girl who whispered, "Good luck," towards me as she walked away.

As he sat down, I could tell he was excited to be here. He just talked and talked.

He introduced himself and said his name was "Ayden Isaiah Holguin Gil,"

I just acknowledged him and thought, *Even this conquistador has two names.*

The girl he walked in with sat a couple of rows away. I figured he had already annoyed her on the first day of school.

This kid was going to struggle to make friends here. I thought to myself.

I heard the late ball ring. I noticed the teacher walking in. She began taking attendance, "Xavier Barrera," she said.

"Present."

"Nice to meet you, Xavier," he said as he turned around.

Once done, Ms. Maynard walked to the front of the classroom and began discussing assignments. There was no introduction, no icebreakers, nothing like that. She handed out a syllabus and instructed us to read a book because we would write an essay.

I didn't want to be here, and as much as I hated being home, it was better than being in this classroom right now. I was too depressed to care about reading. Plus, I could never focus long enough on a story, so they never ended up making sense. Also, I found that most stories were not relatable and used words I didn't understand.

She announced that there would be a parent night in the next following weeks and encouraged us to talk to the school counselor. In case we ever needed to use any counseling resources they had at school.

The rest of the class was just a blur. Nothing stood out. That was until lunchtime.

They were serving a spicy chicken sandwich. That was my favorite, and I knew it would be my favorite part of today.

I saw a table filled with what I assumed were other Mexicans. I saw Ayden sitting at a table by himself. He waved and smiled at me. I just gave him a head nod and tried to avoid him.

I sat at the table, and they all turned and faced me.

"Que onda, paisa," I heard one say.

"Nada," I responded.

They didn't ask me any questions, and then they continued talking.

I knew they were talking in Spanish, but then they started using words that I had never heard before, they were talking about whether or not their trucks "queman," I also heard "placoso, carnal, feto, takuache, buchón, chilo, yunke,"[174] and after every sentence, they would say, "todo bien."

I tried to decipher what they were saying, but I wasn't accustomed to this. I was Mexican, but maybe they were a different type of Mexican. Maybe this was not the right table for me. I just finished my sandwich in silence until lunch was over.

After lunch, I had an art class. Intro to drawing with Mr. Paulson. I was somewhat excited about that class. It sounded foreign and new. I had taken art classes before, but we mostly worked on doodles, no technical work.

That was until I saw Ayden there. When we made eye contact, he softly hit the chair next to him, like he was inviting me to sit next to him. Despite not wanting to, I decided to sit next to him. I might as well sit next to somebody I know, rather than a stranger.

---

[174] Spanish slang

Our art instructor went on about how we would have to paint an entire canvas by the end of the year and start thinking about ideas.

I saw Ayden jotting down notes. What kind of nerd takes notes in art class? For the rest of the class period, we learned the names of specific brushes and when to use them. Pretty uninteresting class.

When the bell rang, I went to history class. I didn't say bye to Ayden and didn't see him again after that.

After school, I got on the bus to go home. I sat by the window. I didn't try to pay attention to anybody. Even though it was August, it was getting cloudy.

Suddenly, I felt an overwhelming rush of sadness. I couldn't explain what was happening. I just needed to get off the bus. Moments later, the bus stopped, and I just got off. It wasn't even my stop, but I just had to. I ran home. I could feel the tears coming down my cheek. After I got tired, I stopped running and began walking, but the tears continued.

Eventually, I made it home. I saw my mom, and she saw that I had been crying. She just looked at me and asked me if everything was okay. I didn't have the words, so I stood there, unable to communicate. I didn't know what I was feeling, and I didn't know how to explain it.

My mom just hugged me. She asked me how school was. I told her that I was thinking about transferring.

"¿A dónde?"[175]

I just shrugged my shoulders.

She wanted to understand why I wanted to move. Was it too difficult, were the people not nice? What made me not want to go there?

"No sé ama."[176]

She crossed her arms, and I knew she would begin lecturing me. I hated it when she did that. She started talking, but I managed to look her in the eyes and just zone her out. I

---

[175] To where?
[176] I don't know.

didn't catch much. I just heard her say, "Más puede el que quiere, que el que puede."[177]

I just nodded and put my backpack down, and she asked me if I had any homework. I shook my head, but she still went through my backpack. She saw the flyer I had gotten earlier.

She looked at it and suggested I might consider going to the counselor since I couldn't talk to her.

That's when I decided I was done talking and just went up to my room.

---

[177] Those who want to go further than those who can.

Hopes and Dreams

I don't recall much from the next couple of days. It was all just a blur. I remember my mom saying she received a phone call about a "Parent's Night." I wish that was one of the phone calls she had ignored or gone to voicemail since our voicemail was full, so nobody could leave any messages.

She asked me if I knew anything about that.

I just shrugged and walked up to my room.

The next morning she told me she was taking me to school. I didn't understand why I had already become familiar with going on the bus, and I had been getting there on time.

She parked her car in front of the school. She didn't take me to the parent drop-off section but instead walked me to the front office. I thought I was in trouble or something. I saw my mom's face, she looked concerned. She asked the front office about "Parent's Night." They told her it would be that night and that she was encouraged to come. It would allow parents to talk to teachers and get to know the school.

I didn't understand why she had been so worried about me. I had always been a decent student, and it had been a while since I had gotten in trouble. I had small issues, mostly warnings for not being able to sit down for long periods and for tapping my pencil, but that was it.

My mom began writing down some notes and assured them she would be there. Then she turned to me, told me to have a good day, and kissed me.

I walked to class and sat in the open seat beside Ayden. We weren't friends, but he would always save me a seat. We wouldn't talk, and sitting next to him during lunch was better than sitting down with the other Mexican kids.

During lunch, he asked me, "Are you coming to Parent's night tonight?"

"Yeah, my mom wants to come. Are you?"

"Yeah, I'm volunteering. I'm helping showcase what this school has to offer and assisting any parents who may have any questions."

I don't know what he wanted out of this interaction, I just knew that he was weird.

Who does that?

"That's cool," I said, trying to be nice.

After school, I got home and asked my mom if I had to go with her. She insisted I did, so I had to go with her.

Even though I didn't want to, I joined her. When we got there, I wasn't relaxed. It felt awkward to be at school with my mom.

I guided her to every class I had; eventually, we ran into Ayden.

"Hey, Xavier," he said.

I could see my mom semi-smile and ask if I could introduce her.

I told her, "This is Ayden. I have a couple of classes with him."

"We also eat lunch together," he butted in.

We walked away, and my mom asked me if we were friends.

"No, Mom, we're not friends; we just have class together."

We continued to go to my classes. Just like Ayden, I saw my mom taking notes. She wrote down information about our English essay and the art project.

She even asked about any upcoming projects we had in math.

"No, there are no math projects. Students will just gradually learn deeper math concepts."

My mom wrote that down. I just thanked Mr. Ashton and left his classroom.

At the end of the tour, I saw my mom walking toward the principal and asking about the school counselor. She was directed to a woman, and she began to speak to her.

Noriega

They chatted for a few minutes and then we returned to the car.

It was a short drive, we didn't talk, and the radio was off. I just looked out the window and got hit with a ray of light every time we passed under a street light.

We pulled into the driveway, and as I tried getting off, my mom began talking.

One of the school's counselors reached out to my mom and suggested that I go visit her the following week.

I did not agree with her on this.

I asked my mom why she was so interested in getting to know all of my teachers and what was going on with my classes.

My mom told me that I needed help and that she couldn't help me.

I told her I was fine, I didn't need anything. Plus, I had always been a typical student that occasionally got into trouble.

"I'm just worried about your mental health."

"I'm fine, Mom," I responded.

"Fine? Just fine?" she asked.

There was a pause, "I just want you to be okay and maybe start thinking about your future."

This confused me.

"I am okay," I told her, "And what about my future?"

"Well, you have to start thinking about college or what you want to do when you get older."

We had never really talked about college before.

"Why do you want to talk about college? That's still like four years away, Mom."

"Lo sé, pero..."[178]

I could see the tears beginning to build up in her eyes.

"Xavier, I want you to succeed in whatever you want to do, but I can't help you. I don't know how to. I know you're struggling emotionally, and I know you don't like sharing your emotions. Also, this is all new to me. Credit hours and

---

[178] I know but...

151

AP classes. I have never heard of that. I didn't get an education like you, and I don't want you to struggle like me."

I just sat there.

"If you're successful, that means I was successful," she said.

I didn't know what to say.

"¿Qué quieres ser cuando crezcas?"[179], she asked.

This reminded me of Frijolito, so I deflected and asked her, "What did you want to be when you were younger?"

I saw the nostalgia forming in her eyes. After a short pause, she said, "When I was younger, I always wanted to be a nurse. I feel like it would be an interesting job. You get to help people, and you can see all kinds of things. I don't think it would get boring. Every day would be an adventure, and I bet some days would be stressful, but that comes with any job."

"What else?" I asked.

"I have always thought about being a pilot. When I was little, I would spend all day looking up at the sky and seeing them fly by. I would just sit there and think about who was on that plane and where they were going. Also, I don't know or have met any female pilots."

"Mom, but you're scared of rollercoasters. I don't think you could be a pilot." I responded.

"I know, but sometimes you must overcome your fears to make your dreams a reality."

Once more, it got quiet. My mom looked at me and brought up counseling.

"Es por tu bien,"[180], she said, "I met the counselor tonight, and she seems like a nice person."

I looked at her. Even though I disagreed with what was happening, I guess it was probably a good idea.

"Okay, pues mom, I'll go," I promised, kissing her on the cheek before getting out of the car. She stayed in the car, and I could hear her put on some music. I heard her singing

---

[179] What do you want to be when you're older?

[180] It's for your own good.

along. It made me think of Frijolito, about how much I missed him.

Mexican Feelings

That following Monday, I woke up and didn't want to go to school. I thought about faking being sick, or about any excuse so really. I didn't want to see the counselor. I didn't even know what counselors did. I didn't bring it up as I was eating breakfast. My mom asked me to pass her the salsa. While she ate her eggs, I started playing with my fork. Just scratching up the plate.

"You nervous about going to the counselor?" She asked.

I just looked up at her, "Más o menos."[181]

"A lo mejor te gusta."[182]

I sat there silently thinking, "I highly doubted that, mom. I mean none of my uncles, cousins, Frijolito, or even yourself have ever talked about your feelings. I don't know how to express myself. This is not something Mexicans do. Mexicans don't go to a therapist, mom. We just shove our feelings down and keep moving on. We don't look back, and we don't let those feelings out. Mexican men don't do that, and I want to be a Mexican man, mom."

This is what I wanted to say, but I couldn't. It's not her fault. She grew up not sharing her feelings. It's how she was raised and what she learned from my grandparents, who learned from their parents. I at least understood that she was trying to be different from them. The least I could do was appreciate that.

I hugged her tightly and promised to go to the counselor.

I had to run out since all this talking had made me late. I almost missed the bus, but I made it just in time.

Weirdly enough, I started to have a good feeling about this.

---

[181] More or less.
[182] Maybe you'll like it.

Noriega

Since I was early, I decided to stop by the counselor's office before going to class.

When I got to the front office, I saw kids outside by the reception desk that had been crying. I instantly knew that this was not the place for me.

I was about to turn around when I saw Ayden exiting the door.

"Going to the counselor?" he asked.

"I was thinking about it, but I don't think it's the place for me."

"You should try it out. It can't hurt."

I guess he was right.

I waited for a couple of minutes before getting called up. It wasn't anything special or life-changing. I just had to fill out a form with my name and student ID number.

That was it. It seemed a little odd, but I didn't question the process. The front desk assistant informed me that I would be scheduled in the near future. I was given a late pass, and I walked to class.

In class, Mrs. Maynard, our English teacher, talked about the book we were going to write about. She specified that she didn't want this to be a book report but rather a reflection on our identities.

I didn't know what that meant. I just looked over at Ayden, who seemed to be overly excited.

"I already know what I'm going to write about," he whispered.

I hadn't even started reading the book, and he was already finished and thinking about the next step.

That whole week, any moment I had to myself, I read the book. I read during lunch since it was better than sitting in silence with Ayden. He would ask me questions and interrupt me. Mainly to see where I was in the book and what I thought about certain parts. I would mostly shrug.

The book focuses on a Native American kid who grew up on a reservation and later moved to a Euro-American high school. It talked about his struggles, but nothing appealed to me.

"You should come over tomorrow, and we can talk about it and work on our essays," he said.

I thought about it, I wasn't sure, but I was struggling with this assignment.

"Sure," I responded.

El Corazón de Melón

I felt the sunlight rays hit my face. It wasn't my favorite way of waking up, but it was better than waking up with a loud alarm or my mom turning on my room light. I hated waking up that way, but it sure was effective. My favorite was waking up to the smell of my mom making breakfast.

After brushing my teeth, I did my best to get my legañas[183] out.

I walked down and saw my mom was already enjoying her cafecito. I gave her a morning kiss and hug and then told my mom that I was going to a classmate's house to work on an essay after school that day.

"¿Un amigo?"[184]

"A classmate mom."

"Ayden?" she asked.

"So, can I go or not?"

With a smirk on her face, she just nodded and asked me not to be late.

I knew she was making a bigger deal than what it was.

That day I walked into class and sat down in my self-assigned seat. I saw Ayden walk in, once again with the girl that had whispered "good luck" at me once. I wonder if they took the same bus since they always walked in together. Before he even sat down, he asked if my mom had given me permission.

"Yeah," I told him.

I could tell he was thrilled about our essay project.

I just looked at him and started to have second thoughts about this.

---

[183] Eye Boogers
[184] A friend?

The rest of the class began to drag, and I felt edgy. I couldn't help it anymore and wanted to get up and walk around. Ms. Maynard thought this was odd, but she just kept teaching. I was just pacing back and forth. I was still paying attention to what was going on.

Once class was over, she asked me to stay in class to discuss what was happening. I told her I just didn't like sitting for long periods of time. She handed me a Rubik's cube.

"This might help stimulate yourself while you sit."

I had seen them before. I didn't know how to solve them, but I understood their concept. All the colors had to match on every side. I started playing with it as I walked into my next class late.

Unfortunately, it was later taken away in Math class. Apparently, it was a distraction.

I got it back after class, but I understood that it was seen as more of a toy, not a tool that kept me focused.

After a quiet lunch where I avoided Ayden, I went into art class.

That day we were going to go over shading and the emphasis on making our art look more "Alive on the page," as Mr. Paulson would say.

When I sat down, Ayden asked me where I had been.

"I went to the counselor during lunch."

"How did you like it?"

"I don't want to talk about it."

I felt rude, but I was uncomfortable talking about the counselor, even if it was a made-up appointment.

After drawing and shading for an hour, we put our books away and waited for the bell. Once it rang, Ayden told me where to meet up after school. I promised him I would be there, and he told me not to be late.

"I won't," I assured him.

"Actually, I might be late. I have to run by my coding class and turn in an assignment."

Who takes a computer class? I wondered, *If you know how to use Google, you're fine.*

After my history class, I considered faking being sick or going home instead. I didn't know what I was going to do. I couldn't ghost him.

That would be rude, I thought, wondering, *How bad could this actually be?*

I walked up to the parent pick-up line and saw him standing there waiting for me. I could sense his excitement from the other side of campus.

As we waited and I asked him how his assignment went, "Great," he responded, "I just had to implement Fibonacci's sequence and use Big O notation to find the time complexity of my solution. You know something rudimentary."

I regretted asking. This sentence took me back to my first day of school.

After that, I saw him wave down a van. I could not believe he would get into a van, but then again, I was not surprised. His mom picked us up. The door slid open. Nothing about this was remotely cool.

I sat down and tried to buckle up, but before I could even click my seatbelt, I heard Ayden's Mom say, "Buenas tardes, corazón de melon."[185]

I let go of my seatbelt. It felt like I had been in this situation before, but this time I couldn't chase my mom and tell her how surprised I was. I was far too old for that. I just sat there and stared straight ahead.

"Buenas tardes, ama."

"¿Y la Andrea?"[186]

"Dijo que tenía que hacer un trabajo y que si podías pasar por ella más tarde."[187]

"Está bien, ¿y quién es tu amigo?"[188]

"Xavier."

---

[185] Good afternoon, honey buns.
[186] Where's Andrea?
[187] She has a project and asked if you could pick her up later?
[188] Who is your friend?

159

"Hola buenas tardes," I responded, trying to be polite.

"Ponte el cinturón,"[189] I heard him say to me.

It felt like time had just stayed still, I listened to what he said, but as we drove away I just sat there. It was a weird feeling. I felt like I had been lied to.

Who is this white kid. How does he know Spanish?

None of this made any sense.

---

[189] Put on your seatbelt.

Whiter than White

During the drive, we passed through Frijolito's old trailer park. It was all blocked off by a fence. I could see that city planners were tearing it down and planning on building something new.

"Gentrification," said Ayden when he caught me looking.

"What does that mean?"

"Oh, um, it's just the process of affluent people moving into an urban community and displacing the current residents to build better houses and attract new businesses."

I just stared at him and hoped he would explain it in simpler terms.

He could tell I was confused, "It's just rich people moving into poor communities and kicking poor people out so they can build nicer houses."

His explanation helped me understand, but it also made me sad.

A couple of minutes later, we made it to his house.

It wasn't too far from me, but this neighborhood was definitely where rich people lived.

I grew up thinking I had money, but this family had money. The house was massive, and it looked brand new. All the houses around here did. They had a gate leading to a driveway and a garage that could fit multiple cars inside. This house was elegant.

Once inside, I saw that they had big tiles on the floor. Not the small kind I grew up with. Then I looked outside and saw that he had a pool. Nobody on my block had a pool. We all had to go to the community one. He even had a swing set and a trampoline. His backyard was filled with green grass, unlike mine, with weeds and random dirt patches.

We could play soccer out there, I thought.

He asked me if I wanted to go up to his room to get started. I just nodded my head. Ayden asked his mom if he could fix us a quick snack.

As we left, I looked at his mom and said, "Con permiso."[190]

"Propio," she responded.

We walked upstairs towards his room. All the doors were massive, and they had granite on every countertop. I wondered what his parents did for a living.

We got into his room, and it was spotless. Everything was where it was supposed to be. No clothes on the ground or anything out of place. He didn't have any posters, but he had a couple of figurines on a counter. He did have a massive window with a telescope pointed out towards the sky.

I looked at Ayden, and then I walked to look through the telescope.

"Be careful the sun is still out, and it could damage your retina, and you could get solar keratitis," He warned.

I decided to look at his backyard instead.

"Nice yard; we could play soccer some time."

"I don't like sports, plus that's where my mom's plants are, and there are bugs outside," he said.

"You don't like any of them?"

"I mean, butterflies are fine, but they're still in their cocoons, and bees are okay. I mean, they do a lot for the environment."

"No, I meant sports."

"Oh, well, I like quidditch."

"I have never heard of that before."

He opened up his backpack and took out his class notebook. I followed his example and began to do the same. I reached for my notebook, and the Rubik's cube fell out.

Before Ayden started to play with it. He marveled at it.

---

[190] Excuse me.

"This colorful cube, just like the Scarlet Macaws," he said.

He knew exactly what flips and turns he had to do. It all felt pretty intense. I wanted to ask him to teach me, but I couldn't do much but stare. After two minutes of complete silence, he solved it.

I was impressed.

"Do you know how to solve it?" he asked.

"No."

"It's just a simple maths algorithm I can teach you later."

"Nothing about that looked simple. And it's math, not maths."

"Actually, maths embodies all the different types of math. Like there's geometry, algebra, calculus, trigonometry, etcetera."

What a nerd, I thought to myself.

Ayden's mom walked in with a bowl of snacks. It was various pieces of fruit cut into smaller pieces. She said something about returning to pick up his sister, and that his dad should be home soon, he had a late case.

Also, she had to stop by the consulate to pick up some paperwork.

Ayden just nodded, and I smiled at her. She closed the door before leaving. Something my mom never did.

"What's the consulate?" I asked him.

He looked at me, unsure how to explain it, "Well, it's a Mexican government building here in the United States to help Mexicans who live here or are currently traveling. Like if they need help with their passports or any issues that may arise."

"Oh," I said. I had more questions, but I didn't know how to ask him, but I didn't have to.

"Yeah, she got transferred here from Mexico, and my dad is an immigration lawyer."

"So, she's been working there for a while, I bet," I said.

"No, we just moved here from Mexico a couple of months ago."

Now I had all the questions.

"Wait, you're Mexican? How do you know English?"

"Yeah, I'm Mexican. My sister and I were born in Culiacan. That's where my mom is from. But my dad was born in Jalisco." he said, "But he was raised in el Distrito Federal."

I had no idea where any of these places were, but he continued speaking before I could ask him.

"And I learned English in school back home. How did you learn English?" he asked.

He was still fixated on the Rubik's cube. I looked at him. I mean, look at him. He didn't like soccer. He rarely spoke any Spanish; from what I saw, he liked computers, art, and other stuff. Ayden was even less Mexican than me, but he didn't seem to care.

He finished solving the cube for the 7th time in a row. He handed it back and looked at me. I bet he could see the shock on my face.

He finally brought up the book, but I was not interested in that. I wanted to get to know him more. I actually wanted to talk to him more.

"But you're white, eres un gringo," I said.

He just moved his head back. It was like a mental flinch. He looked at me like he was studying me. I wondered what my face said.

"No, I'm not. If anything, you're lighter than me," he told me.

"No, I'm not," I responded, mildly offended.

"Yeah, you are."

"Naw, aw."

And just like that, we had become first graders arguing about skin color. In a way it made me realize why racism is such a complex issue. I realized then that even though I was not racist, the idea of being prejudiced toward people with different skin tones was engraved in me.

Noriega

"Yes, you are; your skin complexion is lighter than mine. I spend less time in the sun, so I'm less tan. Also, my eye color makes me look lighter too."

I wanted to confirm his theory, but I didn't know how.

Finally, he said, "Take off your shoes and socks."

I don't know why, but I listened to him. He did the same, and then we compared.

He was right.

We heard somebody walking inside. I wondered who it was.

Ayden's mom popped her head inside.

She caught us both without any socks, comparing ourselves.

"I'm darker than him, huh," he asked her for confirmation.

She told us that she didn't want to be involved and just walked away. After hearing all this commotion, his sister walked in.

I looked at her in awe. She was in my English class. She was the girl I always saw him coming into class with, the one that warned me about him.

"I told you to stay away," she joked.

"Come down for dinner," I heard somebody say. I just stayed put with Ayden until I figured out what to do.

"She's your sister?"

"Yeah, we're twins."

The amount of information I could process in one day had been met. This was all too much for me.

"Want to stay for dinner?" he asked.

"I can't. I promised my mom I wouldn't be home late."

As we walked downstairs, I saw his father sitting at the table. He shook my hand and asked me who I was. I explained the best I could. He invited me to stay for dinner, but I told him I couldn't. I just wanted to get out of there. As I was walking to the door, he stopped me.

"How are you getting home?"

"On the bus."

"Oh, I see. How long will that take you?"

"About forty minutes, depending on when the bus arrives."

"You could take the bus and get there in approximately 40 minutes, but you will still be hungry."

There was a pause.

"Oh, te puedes quedar a comer y nosotros te llevamos."[191]

I hated his use of logic. It was a fair deal.

The truth was that I didn't want to stay, but now I felt obligated.

I decided to put my backpack down and sit. Even though what I wanted to do was run away.

Ayden and his sister were helping set up the table. They had multiple plates that all matched. There was a familiar smell in the air. I just couldn't pinpoint what it was exactly. It was chicken, chicken with a side of nopales. This confirmed it, they were Mexican.

"¿Te gustan los nopales?"[192]

"No," I said.

They all looked at me like I had killed somebody.

What is it about Mexicans and nopales? Why do they like them so much?

Ayden's family started eating, but I decided to get up. I could feel them staring at me as I washed my hands in the sink. I had never done that before, but I didn't want them to think that I had no manners or was dirty.

I sat down and ate chicken with the rest of them. Ayden's dad began asking me questions about who I was, like my interests and background. I opened up as much as I could. Then Ayden's father asked me about my mom and where she worked. I answered. I was dreading the next question. He asked me about my father.

I just shrugged, "No lo conozco,"[193], I said.

---

[191] Or you can stay, and we'll give you a ride.

[192] You don't like nopales?

[193] I don't know him.

I could sense the awkwardness starting to build up. Ayden's dad panicked about what to say next, so he just asked me if I had any classes with Andrea.

"English, I just didn't know they were brother and sister."

"Cuates,"[194] said Ayden's mother.

I had never heard that word before.

"Yeah, we get that a lot," said Andrea; I just smiled at her and kept eating.

We finished up dinner, and I helped clean up the dishes. After we finished, Ayden's parents gave me a ride home. Actually, everybody got in the car. I was not sure why, but they did. I figured that they were just a close-knit family.

I told them where to turn and where to go, and when we got home, I took off my seatbelt.

Before I got off, Ayden spoke up and said, "Are you coming over tomorrow? We need to start this project before it's too late."

"You guys didn't even work on it?" said his mom in a startled tone, "¿Entonces qué hicieron? I mean, besides looking at each other's feet."

I looked away and started to laugh as I got off. I walked to my front door and turned around to wave at them.

When my mom opened the door, they were gone.

"How did it go?" she asked.

I just smiled at her and walked in.

"You hungry?"

"No, I already ate."

"What did you eat?" she asked.

"Pollo con nopales," I responded.

"¿Nopales?" she said, confused.

"Yeah," I said as I walked towards my room.

---

[194] Fraternal Twins

The Chorizo Test

The following morning, I got up early and ready as fast as possible. My mom was already in the kitchen; I wondered when she got up. She was always ready by the time I sat down at the table.

I told my mom that I was going to be late that night.

"I'm going to Ayden's house because we didn't finish our project."

"Is it because you wasted time getting to know him because he's your friend?" she asked.

"No, ama, he's not my friend. It's just a big project."

Part of me wanted to tell her everything I had learned about him. But I decided not to.

On my way to school, I tried to think about what questions I could ask Ayden to test how Mexican he really was.

I could maybe ask him about Cantiflas or El Chavo del Ocho. Or what the two channels every Mexican television had. Maybe who the current president is. Actually, who is the current president? Maybe I should know that myself.

I began to write down as many questions as I could on a piece of paper.

I got to school and saw Andrea walking down the hallway, "Where's your brother?" I asked her.

"Counseling," she said.

We walked together towards class. We had never talked before. But it was nice having small talks that weren't deep or personal. "Sorry about my parents, they can be metiches,"[195] she said.

"Yeah, it was a little awkward, but don't worry. They were just trying to get to know me."

---

[195] Nosy

It felt good to open up and admit that I wasn't completely comfortable talking about that man.

Ayden didn't make it into English class. I guess I would have to wait until lunch to see him. Before class ended, I approached Andrea and asked her if her brother was okay. "Yeah?" she said, confused. "I think he just had a lot to talk about today."

I began to worry about him.

During lunch, I sat down at the table that we usually sat at. I wasn't interested in eating my slice of pizza. My eyes were just glued to the door. I couldn't see him, and it was like he had disappeared. Maybe he had gone home, but I didn't know where Andrea was, so I couldn't ask her.

Then out of the corner of my eye, I saw him making his way toward me with a smile.

"Is everything okay?" I asked him.

"Yeah, the counselors just had a huge line because they were running late. So, I had to wait my turn, and it took longer than expected, and I had to miss my first period," he explained.

Before he could sit down, I began interrogating him. I pulled out my piece of paper filled with questions, and in rapid succession, I began, "Who is Mexico's president? When was Mexico founded? Who is Cantiflas and la India María? What money is used in Mexico? Who invented the lotería? Who—"

Ayden cut me off, "Are you actually interested, or are you just trying to test how Mexican I am? Because if that's the case, you know there's a better way to do it; it's called "The Chorizo Test". It was created to counterbalance against standardized tests and was used to—"

I couldn't believe it. "Shut up, Ayden", I yelled, laughing, "You human factoid machine."

He just smiled.

I looked at him in disbelief, "Is there anything you don't know?"

"That's an interesting question," He said, "I know that there are some things that I don't know, but I don't know what those things are."

"You're such a nerd," I told him.

"I'm still more Mexican than you."

I wanted to argue with him but didn't have a counterpoint.

"Are you still coming over to work on your essay?"

I nodded my head.

After lunch, we walked together to art class. I could tell he absolutely loved that class. To me, it was about making doodles and just perfecting them. To him, it was something more. Something I could not fully understand.

We met up, after school. Ayden's sister, Andrea, was already waiting. I had spent so much time thinking about Ayden that I never paid her any attention. I wondered what her days looked like; I wouldn't see her around school after first period.

Ayden caught me staring at his sister. He just smiled at me.

"You know if you think my sister is cute you also think I'm cute. By default of course due to the fact that we have the same genetics. We share 50 percent of our DNA. Did you know—"

"Ayden, I'm not checking out your sister", I said nudging him and awkwardly smiling at Andrea,

Thankfully, Ayden's mom pulled up. After a quiet ride, we went straight to his room, and for some reason, I actually wanted to talk about the assignment. I was interested in hearing Ayden's thoughts about it. Unfortunately, that is not what happened, and we got up there and started writing. His mom brought up snacks and let us continue working.

"Do you want to write down ideas and talk about them once we finish our rough drafts?" he asked.

"Sure," I said.

I had no clue what I was going to write about. I skimmed the book. I mean, I had read it, but nothing stood out.

I looked at the main character's family dynamics and his schooling, but it was all different than mine. Nothing seemed to be connected.

The main character in this book had a tough life. I have not had a challenging life, but we are not entirely different. His teacher saw so much potential in him and didn't want him to waste it. We are not completely the same, but he had to go to a new school. He was not sure, and I was unsure too. So, we are the same. The main character is sad to go to his new school. I was sad coming here too.

After writing for 30 minutes, I showed him my work so he could give me feedback.

He looked puzzled. "Why is it formatted like that? And why is it so short?" he asked, "Additionally, is that all you really think you both have in common?"

"Let me see yours then."

"No, I'm not finished, and I don't like people seeing my unfinished work."

"Well then, what else do I have in common then?"

"You're both indigenous, well the author says "Indian," but I prefer the word "Indigenous." Plus, you are both searching for an identity. I would expand on that trauma."

"Indigenous? Trauma?" I asked. How did this Mexican kid know more English words than me?

"Well, Indigenous just means that you are native to the land like your ancestry is from this land."

"My mom is from Mexico."

"Yeah, I understand, but you are native to the Americas."

I was getting confused. I couldn't understand, and I could see Ayden getting frustrated due to his inability to explain what he wanted to tell me.

171

He took a deep breath and gathered his ideas, "Look, you're Mexican, right?"

"Yes, I am Mexican," I think that was the first time I had admitted that to myself.

"It doesn't matter what region of Mexico you are from. There is some Indigenous blood in you. For example, the most commonly found in Mexico is Nahua. The Aztecs and Toltecs, who had empires all over central and southern Mexico, were considered Nahua, so they spoke Nahuatl."

"They didn't speak Spanish?"

Ayden just looked at me like I was dumber than he originally had thought. He didn't know if he should go off topic and give me a quick lesson on the history of language in Mexico or just finish this lecture.

"Anyways, they are Indigenous. They are mostly found in southern Mexico or Central America. Then there are also Mayan people. As you move further north, you have the Mixtec, Otomi, Zapotec, Mazatec, and Tzotzil."

"These are all like Mexican Indians, right?"

"Yes, Mexican Indigenous people, then in Northern Mexico and some of Southern United States, we have Apache and Yaqui."

"How can Mexican Natives also be American?"

"They were there before the border was up. Long before their land became part of the United States."

"The United States used to be part of Mexico?"

"Yeah, it was stolen."

"Stolen? Which parts?"

"Arizona, California, New Mexico, Texas, Colorado, Nevada, and Utah."

"We used to be part of Mexico?" I asked.

"Yes," he responded.

The more I learned, the more I was embarrassed. I didn't know any of this. I didn't realize how ignorant I was before.

"Why wasn't I taught any of this?"

"You probably were, but it was probably sugar-coated. It was called "The Treaty of Guadalupe Hidalgo," and the United States paid 15 million dollars for the land they took."

"So, it wasn't stolen then."

"Mexico was forced to sell. They went to war, and after we lost, it was stolen."

I didn't know what to do with all this information. I realized I was more than just Mexican; I was also Indigenous.

I continued to work on my essay. Maybe I did have more in common with this character than I had thought. I was Indigenous, just like him, and I was still searching for my identity.

El Cubo de Rubik

"C+"

That's the grade I got on my essay. I looked at it. It was beautiful. I had never been more proud of such a low grade before.

Ayden looked at my score, "Sorry, man, I tried to help you the best I could."

"It wasn't you. My writing just sucks."

"Yes, your writing does need to improve, especially when it comes to cohesively developing your ideas."

Why did he talk like that?

We quickly moved on from that conversation.

"Do you have any plans for tomorrow?"

"Plans? Me? No."

"You want to come over? I can help you solve your Rubik's Cube."

I was hesitant, but I told him I had not asked my mom for permission. It wasn't that I didn't want to. I just didn't know if I could.

"I haven't asked my mom, and I don't want to go without permission because she'll worry about me more than she already does."

He took that as an acceptable excuse.

Five minutes before the bell, I got a slip; it read "Counselor" at the top. Ayden was too distracted to notice me getting up and leaving the class period. I wanted to say bye. I just didn't know how to.

As I was going, I suddenly became very nervous. I had been ignoring thinking about this for a while, and I had completely forgotten about it.

When I walked to the front office, I saw the counselor waiting for me at her door, and she apologized for not being able to meet with me earlier and introduced herself.

Noriega

"Hello, my name is Avery Jimenez. I look forward to getting to know each other."

This was the first time I had made eye contact with her. I was surprised by her demeanor. She wasn't an older lady. It was weird. Maybe slightly older than my mom, but not old enough to be my grandma. She had nice wavy hair, darker in color. I could see some wrinkles forming as she smiled.

"I just wanted to introduce myself before I see you on Friday before school."

"Okay," I said, "I'll write it on my calendar."

There was no way I would forget, but I didn't know what else to say. I could already tell how awkward I was being.

During lunch, Ayden asked me where I had gone. I showed him the slip I had gotten earlier.

"Oh, I see. How did it go?"

"Fine," I said.

"Well, if you ever want to talk about it, let me know."

I saw Andrea approach the table, and she greeted me.

"Hey, Xavier."

She turned to her brother, "Ayden, are you ready? My mom's already here, and if you don't hurry, we're going to be late to our dentist appointment."

"Yeah, sorry, Xavier, we won't be creating masterpieces in art today."

That made me laugh. What a strange thing to say.

"Later, Ayden and Andrea."

"Yeah, and don't forget to ask your mom about tomorrow."

"I won't," I promised.

That day when I got home, I told her a little more about Ayden, and what I got on the essay.

"You got a C?"

"A C+, Mom."

"It's the same," she said.

I wanted to make my case, but then I remembered that I wanted permission to go to his house.

"You want to go over? Why? Do you have another project to work on?" she asked jokingly.

"No, just to hang out."

"Xavier has a friend," she said, teasing me.

"Mom, I'm not in preschool anymore, and if you keep this up, people will never want to be my friend."

"You can go, pero te portas bien."[196]

"I promise," I told her before kissing her on the cheek and going to shower.

"Oh, and I am meeting with the counselor on Friday."

"Wait, what? On Friday?"

"Bye, Mom, I love you," I yelled as I went to my room.

The following day I saw Andrea. I went up to her and asked her about Ayden. She pointed back, and I saw him walking up. He seemed distracted in his own thoughts.

"Thanks," I said to her.

I yelled across the hallway, "I asked my mom if I could go over, and she said yes. But I have to behave myself."

"Yes," he said as he punched the sky, celebrating.

I was going up for a high five, but he hugged me.

I didn't know how to react, so I pushed him away.

He seemed confused, "Are you okay?"

"Yeah, that was just weird."

"Are you homophobic?"

"You know damn well I don't know what that means."

"It means that you have strong prejudice towards gay people."

"What? Me? No."

"Then what is it?"

"I don't know. I don't think I've ever had another boy hug me."

"What about your da…." He stopped himself before he could finish that statement.

"Yeah…" I looked at him and did a half-smile.

---

[196] Be on your best behavior.

We walked into class, changing the subject. It was still a little awkward.

"Anyways, my mom said I could go."

I avoided him during lunch and sat next to him during art.

"I'm sorry," he said as I sat down.

"Don't worry about it."

I looked over at his art and saw that he was very talented, unlike me.

After school, we met up at the usual location. Andrea was already there. We both just stood there, and as soon as Ayden arrived, their mom pulled up. Andrea sat in the front while we both sat in the back.

When we got there, we went up to his room.

I could tell things between us were still a little bit weird. So, I decided to break the silence.

"How do you like therapy?"

"I think it's been helping me," he said. "Have you been liking therapy? Have you been able to see positive results yet?"

"I haven't gone yet. I have my first session on Friday."

"I thought you said that you had been going."

"I lied."

"Why did you lie?"

"We weren't friends then."

"So, you're saying we're friends?"

"Man, you sound just like my mom."

"It's okay. I haven't been able to make a friend since I've been here."

That made me sad.

"Why have you been going to therapy?"

I could tell that he was a little uncomfortable with that question. Ayden seemed to tense up.

"To relieve my niggling depression."

"Niggling?" I asked.

"Yeah, niggling means to cause slight but persistent anxiety."

"So, what caused you to have depression?" I asked.

It was quiet for a few moments. He didn't speak, and I didn't know how to push him.

"Well… ", He began, "Before we moved here, I was really excited when I learned that my mom was getting transferred. The idea of moving to a new country sounded like an adventure. I was thrilled to start a new life in a new place. I didn't have a lot in common with the people back home. I have always had different interests. It sounded perfect, but then I found out that my grandma was sick. My grandpa, Pedro, had already passed away when we were younger, so we were all she had. She was my biggest fan; she loved everything I did, and whenever I shared something new, she told me that I reminded her so much of my grandpa. I don't remember him, I never got to meet him, but I've seen pictures of him. He had an identical twin, so I know exactly what he would have looked like, thanks to my tío Toribio."

Toribio? I thought to myself. *What a weird name.*

I could sense a sadness in his voice.

"My parents put their plans to move on hold, which was nice for me since I loved my grandma so much, but she passed away in her sleep a couple of weeks later. The last time I saw her, she couldn't remember who I was, and I don't think I recovered from that. Then a couple of months later, when we were leaving, my mom told me we had to leave my dog, Capitan, behind. My mom said he was too old and that it would be better for him to just spend his time peacefully at home. I never got to see him again. I began to feel guilty for leaving. I didn't know what to do. My parents suggested I go to counseling. So, I did. I'm not saying it's a cure. But it is better than what I was doing."

I looked at him and thought, *Damn, he really does need this*, and wondered, *If this is what I needed too?*

"What about your sister?" I asked.

Noriega

"No, she didn't take it as hard as I did. I'm the emotional one out of the two. She found a way to cope with it better than I did."

"Cope?"

"Yeah, like, deal with it. I wasn't always a good artist or into art. But it helps me express myself. Helps me show my feelings and deal with my trauma"

I had heard that word repeatedly. "Trauma", and it reminded me of my talks with Frijolito, only this was different. It was depressing.

"Why do you need therapy?" he asked.

"Trauma," I said.

La Quinceañera

I desperately wanted the subject to change. I didn't know what to say, but luckily, Andrea walked into the room.

"Do you want to wear lime green or turquoise?"

"I thought we agreed on red."

"Yeah, but I don't think I like it."

I was just sitting there confused. I didn't know what was going on. They both got quiet and began looking at me.

"We're planning our quinceañera," she said.

"You're planning our quinceañera." Ayden corrected her.

"I thought quinceañera was just for girls," I said.

"Well, traditionally—" began Ayden before he was interrupted by Andrea yelling out, "Byeeeeeeeee!"

Andrea understood that Ayden was about to go into a history lesson and decided to run out of the room as soon as possible. However, I was excited about these learning opportunities.

"Oh, okay Andrea, Bye. Did Mom call out? Or is dinner ready?" he asked, confused.

Andrea stopped at the door, unsure of what to say.

I felt like he didn't understand why she was leaving, but I didn't want to be the one to explain it to him.

"Yeah, I heard your mom call her name," I said.

She just smiled at me before heading out.

"So quinceañeras?" I asked.

"Like I was saying," he began, "Quinceañeras are traditionally for women. Or girls who are beginning their journey into womanhood."

"So, you're becoming a woman?" I asked sarcastically.

"No pendejo," he responded in a snappy tone.

I laughed. I had never heard him use language like that before.

Noriega

I looked at him and said, "Qué bonito vocabulario."[197]

He just rolled his eyes and continued talking, "It is a tradition, it used to symbolize that women were ready to get married, but it has just become a symbolic journey. Now there is some debate about where they originated from. Some believe it was brought by the Spanish when they came to Mexico. Others believe it was already an Aztec celebration since the Aztecs were astronomers and did a phenomenal job keeping track of time."

He took a slight pause. I knew he was about to hit me with some knowledge. I loved how his face lit up when he talked about something he was enthusiastic about.

I pretended to start taking notes and saw him laughing.

"If you want to take notes, did you know Aztecs had two calendars? One had 365 days and kept track of the solar year, while another only had 260. The second one, called Tonalpohualli, was used to keep track of various rituals. They also had Aztec Zodiac signs to go along with it, where each symbol lasted 13 days, so they had 20 signs total. I used to know the name of all 20, but now I can only remember Ocelotl, Ollin, Xochitl, Calli, Acatl, Coatl, and Atl. Oh, and then there is Cipactli, Ehecatl, Cuetzpalin, Miquiztli, Mázatl, Itzcuintli, Ozomahtli and Malinalli. I know that I'm forgetting some. Anyways, every 52 years, when the two calendars would align, the Aztecs became superstitious and believed that the world would end on that day. Therefore, they would have a "New Fire Ceremony." They had all types of ceremonies."

I just kept pretending to write as it got quiet. He knew a lot about everything. I didn't even know how this was possible.

"What else do you know about them?" I asked.

"Well, besides all of the ceremonies, they were pretty brutal. They would sacrifice up to twenty thousand people a year. Aztecs had sophisticated forms of slavery," he said, disheartened like he was ashamed of it.

---

[197] That's not very appropriate vocabulary.

181

"What do you love about them, though?" I asked.

"Well, they loved sports. They had their own version of soccer. Well, it was a mix of soccer and basketball. It was called ōllamalitzli. Aztecs were very competitive."

"Sports? You don't even like sports."

I know, well, Aztecs had a big love for art. They would make sculptures, pottery, poems, and music. They have a famous creation story about how music was created."

"Music? Poems?" I said as I wrote it down.

"Yeah, but Aztecs were skilled architects. They built huge pyramids, like Templo Mayor, and were excellent accountants. They even invented chocolate."

"Chocolate?"

"Yeah, Aztecs believed that chocolate was a gift from the gods. To them, it was considered more valuable than gold. They would use it as currency. There is even a rumor that the Aztec emperor Montezuma II would drink gallons of this daily. That it gave him special powers," he said with his eyes wide open. He was more impressed than me, and he already knew this.

"Jewelry was also popular. Aztecs would pierce their faces, like their nose and ears. They would even pierce their teeth."

"Teeth?" I said, astonished.

"Yeah, they would fill their teeth with precious stones, like jade. They would do all types of stuff like that. After battles, they would give you tattoos if you survived and came back home. The more tattoos a person had, the greater a warrior they were seen as. They didn't have quinceañeras to become men."

"So why are you having one?"

"Oh, it's just that Andrea and I are twins, and she's having one. It would be weird if they did that for her, and I just got a birthday cake. It has just become a celebration of traditions. You know, she will get her last doll because she's no longer a child, and her first dance, I wonder what I'll get. Maybe a Hot Wheel or something like that."

Noriega

He paused briefly, then said, "I know it's silly, but it's a tradition."

A tradition, I thought to myself as I wondered, *What traditions we had in my family.*

"It'll be in Mexico next summer if you want to stop by. In Culiacán."

"I'll have to see," I said.

"Oh, and Tochtli, Cuauhtli, Cozcaquautli, Tecpatl, and Quiáhuitl were the other Aztec zodiac symbols."

He never ceased to impress me. Ayden might have been the smartest person I knew. Even when he was talking nonstop, he could still recall the names he was missing. I couldn't even remember everything he had just told me.

I just smiled and said, "The Aztecs were impressive people. I can see why you descended from them"

"Yeah, cause I'm an ocēlōtl,"[198] he said, "And you're a cuāuhtli[199]. Going to therapy takes courage," he said, bumping my shoulder with his fist.

I thought about what he said. I didn't know what those words meant, but I was grateful for Ayden. He was a really good friend to have.

---

[198] Jaguar warrior
[199] Eagle warrior

El Grito

The next day, I was standing in front of the counselor's door. I just looked at the name tag. Avery Jimenez. There was no walking back. Since she was already at the door waiting on me.

"Welcome," she said as she made me sit in a chair. I didn't know what to say. She just started writing in her notebook. I was uncomfortable. I didn't know what to say.

"I can assure you I'm not suicidal," I said jokingly.

She just started writing faster. I could hear myself screaming inside my head, *"What the hell are you writing?"*

She asked me, "Why do you think you're here?"

I thought about it for a second. I didn't want to joke around anymore.

"I don't know how to explain it, but I have these episodes of darkness. Like I am not depressed, but I just feel something heavy. I can't escape it. It is not that I want to feel this way. Sometimes I can feel it creeping up, like walking into a room or on my way home. Then I'll just feel it weighing over me."

She just sat there writing steadily, "What are you running away from?"

I just shrugged.

"What is it that you don't want to feel?"

"I don't want to feel this."

"What do you mean by this? Depression?"

"I don't have depression."

"Depression isn't always about being sad. Sometimes it is the inability to express how we feel. Either because you don't feel comfortable or because you haven't been given the tools to succeed."

I don't know why, but that made me feel better.

Noriega

"You have an assignment. Next time you come, I want you to tell me what makes you feel this way."

It felt like a short meeting. I wrote down what she asked me to in a notebook and closed my backpack.

"Thanks for coming," she said, holding the door open.

It felt sincere, but it didn't make me feel happy.

I walked back to class. By this time, it was close to first period. It was a lot to process, so when I saw Ayden, I told him I was not ready to discuss this. He acknowledged this and asked me if I was excited about September 16th.

"No?" I said, confused. I didn't know what that date was or why it was important. It wasn't his birthday? Was it?

I looked at him but was distracted by a flyer on the wall. It was for upcoming soccer tryouts, and there it was, that niggling feeling I was beginning to get too familiar with. I stopped what I was doing and wrote it down. Writing it down didn't stop that feeling from coming, but I knew I would have something to share next time.

Later during art class, I saw Ayden be his usual self. Overly excited about the canvass, the paintbrushes, and the colors.

"I need to start working on my project. I want to create something that symbolizes and gives tribute to my roots."

"That project is due in May," I reminded him.

"I know, but did you know that the Mona Lisa took 4 years to paint? I don't have four years."

There was a pause.

"So, are you going to try out for soccer?" he asked.

"I don't know. Why'd you ask?"

"I saw you looking at the flyer."

I didn't know what to say. I just wanted to change the subject.

"What's on September 16th?" I asked.

"That's Mexico's Independence Day."

"I thought it was Cinco de Mayo."

Ayden looked at me like I was an idiot. I knew he wanted to smack me in the head.

I didn't know what to say, so I asked, "So what's Cinco de Mayo?"

"It's when Mexico defeated France."

I was confused. I think Ayden knew me well enough to know that I needed more information than just that. I just stared at him until he began talking.

"Okay, well, when Mexico was a new country, they owed a lot of money to France, Britain, and Spain. Those countries decided to send military ships and infantry to get their money back. Benito Juárez, the president at the time, was also the first Indigenous president of Mexican descent—"

"A native." I said, interrupting his flow,

"Yes, Indigenous." He corrected me, "Anyways, Spain and Britain negotiated with Mexico and took their troops, but France didn't. French Emperor Napoleon III decided to attack. He used the debt as an excuse but wanted to expand his Empire in Latin America. He sent 6,000 men, and Mexico only had about 2,000. The French poorly executed the attack, and brave Mexican soldiers stood their ground. After a day of being bombarded, the Mexican army fought back and eventually won."

"Why is it celebrated here, I asked?"

The bell rang before he could say another word, and we all had to pack up.

"Sorry, I have a maths exam next period," he said, leaving.

He left his art supplies out, so I put them away for him. I looked inside his notebook and saw sketches of an eagle, some of a jaguar, one that looked like a snake, and one that resembled a nectar-feeding insect.

I went home that day. I wanted to know more about "September 16th," since it was only a few weeks away.

When I got home, my mom asked me about therapy.

"¿Cómo te fue?"[200]

---

[200] How did it go?

"Bien," I said, "I'll continue going, but I'm just not comfortable talking about it with you right now."

I could see the sadness on her face, especially in her eyes, but she understood.

I asked her, "What's September 16th."

She looked at me confused, "Es el día de la independencia de México."[201]

"Y ¿Qué pasa?"[202]

"Dan el grito."[203]

"¿El Grito?" I asked.

"El presidente grita "Viva"[204] que fue empezado por Miguel Hidalgo Y Costilla."

It was quiet for a few seconds.

So Mexicans yell "Viva"[205] on Independence Day, I thought.

"Me gustaría ir,"[206] I said.

"Háblale a tu nana, para ver si van a haber celebraciones este año y vamos."[207]

"Really?"

"Yeah, why not?"

I entered the kitchen and asked her to dial my grandma's number.

I could hear the phone ringing. It always rings differently when I call somebody in Mexico. After a few moments, my grandma answered.

"Hola nana. Buenas noches, ¿Cómo estás?"

"¿Xavier?" she said delightedly. I heard her cough in the background.

"Si nana ¿Y mi tata?"[208]

---

[201] Mexico's Independence Day?

[202] And what happens?

[203] A celebration that proclaims Mexico's independence and greatness.

[204] The president yells Viva.

[205] Long Live

[206] I'd like to go,

[207] Call your grandma to see if there will be any celebrations this year.

[208] Yes grandma, where's my grandpa?

"Salió a la tienda, ¿Cómo te fue hoy?"[209]

"Bien fui con una terapeuta."[210]

"¿Te lastimaste? ¿Qué te duele? ¿Qué musculo?"[211]

"No nana, no a ese tipo de terapeuta, fui con una psicóloga."[212]

¿Psicóloga? ¿Y eso por qué mijito? ¿Estás bien, te paso algo? ¿Estás enfermo? ¿Estás loco?"[213] her tone shifted. I could hear that she was concerned.

I was confused, "¿No?" I didn't know why she had reacted like this.

"Nana," I said, "¿Nomas para platicar con alguien?"[214] "¿Necesitas ayuda?"[215]

I didn't know how to answer that, so there was silence, and I decided to continue the conversation. "¿Van a ver celebraciones el 16 de septiembre?"[216]

She was concerned. I could hear it in her voice, "Si. ¿Por qué?"[217]

"Me gustaría ir."[218]

"A bueno, si aquí van a ver celebraciones."[219]

"A bueno gracias, nana. Hasta luego."[220]

"Gracias mijito, cuídate, por favor, lo quiero mucho. Voy a rezar por ti."[221]

I didn't know how to react, "Gracias," I said rather awkwardly.

I wondered, *"Why was she would pray for me?"*

---

[209] He went to the store, how was your day today?

[210] Good I went to therapy.

[211] Therapy? Are you injured? What muscle did you hurt?

[212] No grandma, not that type of therapy, I went to a psychologist.

[213] Psychologist? Why are you okay? Are you crazy?

[214] It's just for me to have somebody to talk to.

[215] Do you need help?

[216] Are there going to be celebrations on the 16th of November?

[217] Yes, why?

[218] I would like to go.

[219] Okay, yeah there are going to be festivities.

[220] Thanks grandma, I'll talk to you soon.

[221] Thanks, take care I love you and I'll pray for you.

"Que dios me lo bendiga. Pásame a tu mama por favor."[222]

"A bueno pues gracias, la quiero mucho, bye."

I passed the phone to my mom, who was standing there. I felt a little ashamed about going to therapy. I wondered why my grandma had asked me those questions.

My mom understood what was happening. I heard them talking on the phone. I didn't want to listen to what was being said, so I left the room. After talking, my mom hung up and sat beside me in the living room.

We heard the phone ring, but we both ignored it.

She began talking about her childhood. "Growing up, we used to live on a ranch. We had chickens, turkeys, cows, and one bull. Four different families lived there. All in our own little houses. Growing up, all we had to play with was mud. We would make toys out of mud." she said, laughing. "I played with so much mud that I never wanted to see you having to play with mud. We didn't have a school nearby, so we never got a formal education."

I didn't know where she was going with this.

"Your grandparents, well… they're uneducated. They never went to school. Times were different back then. Now, they're not dumb. Your grandma is a math whiz, but they are just not open-minded about new ideas. But it is not their fault that is just how they were raised and how they grew up. Going to therapy does not mean you're crazy. I think it takes courage to break cycles. You should be proud of yourself. I can't even help you. I just know that you need help."

I needed that. More than I realized. That reassurance. I hugged her tightly.

---

[222] I hope God watches over you; can I talk to your mom please?

Luis Ernesto

The following week, I saw Ayden. I told him I was going to go to Mexico for Independence Day.

"Are you going to throw fireworks in the plaza?"

"They use fireworks? Like on the 4th of July?"

"Yeah, fireworks are not just used here. They're used all over the world."

I always learned something new with Ayden, definitely more than in school. He never made me feel dumb, no matter how little I knew compared to him.

"When's your next appointment."

"Appointment?"

"Yeah, with the counselor."

"Oh, this Friday."

"How are you coming along with your assignment?"

"How do you know about that?"

"She gives everybody an assignment."

I didn't know that. I felt like there had been an invasion of privacy.

"Oh, I've been noting what makes me sad."

"Good, that's healthy," he said.

I spent that whole week looking at what made me sad. Whenever I felt unhappy or gloomy, I just wrote it down.

So there I was, looking at the nameplate, "Avery Jimenez." I stood there for a second, looking at my notebook. She came up to the door and welcomed me in.

We sat there, and she just looked at me.

"Well, how are you feeling?" she asked.

"Good."

"What did you write down? Did you find out anything?"

I looked at my notes and said, "Rain makes me sad. It doesn't even have to be raining. If I smell like it's going to rain, I start to feel heavy. It's not painful like I'm hurting, but more like something is holding me back from being happy. It's almost like I'm lost or something. I don't know if it's the weather or maybe when the sky gets dark. It just gets me depressed."

She began writing notes down, "What else?".

"Sometimes when I am in the car, and certain songs play on the radio, I get sad."

"Are they sad songs?"

"No, not sad songs."

She continued writing.

"Anything else?"

"I saw a soccer tryout flyer."

"Are you planning on trying out?"

I just shook my head.

"What's the pattern here? How do all these instances tie in together?"

"I don't know."

"Your mom spoke to me about Luis Ernesto."

I looked up. I had not heard his name in a while. I had not talked about him or mentioned his name, but that didn't mean I didn't think about him often.

"His name is Frijolito," I whispered.

"Let's talk about him."

For the first time, I did not feel like this was a safe place. I felt betrayed and insecure. I realized then that I was not ready to talk about him. I had lost my best friend, my only brother. When he left, I didn't just lose a person. I lost a part of my childhood and my sense of fun and innocence. I realized what pain was. I kept it to myself, and I had built all these walls I was not ready to bring down.

"I'm not ready for that talk."

"Well, I will be here to talk about it when you are."

I got up, she handed me a late pass, and I walked out. I didn't go back to class. I just went to the nearest bathroom, where I sobbed quietly.

El Torito

A week later, my mom and I packed up for our trip. September 16th fell on a Saturday, so it was the perfect opportunity for us.

She had been asking me all week how I was doing and how therapy was going. I lied to her and told her it was going great. I don't know if she believed me.

We got in the car and began our trip. My mom had already called the school, so my absence was excused.

I had already shared my plans with Ayden, so he knew he wouldn't see me. He was super excited for me, though. I loved that about him. He was always so happy for others.

I was nervous my mom would ask me about what happened in therapy. Like she had been doing all week, but she didn't. It was just a pleasant long drive. I still could not believe we were going to drive for hours just for me to experience this.

After a couple of rest stops filled with snacks and bathroom breaks, we made it. I began to wonder how my mom could go for hours without peeing.

When we got there. I saw my grandma. I had not talked to her since we talked on the phone weeks prior. She was always happy to see us drive up. However, unlike before, she had difficulty getting up. She complained about being tired and mentioned that she was fatigued.

"Ya estoy viejita,"[223] she joked and coughed.

I kissed her, and she smiled and went back to sleep.

Before I could sit down, my mom told me to get ready because we were leaving.

"Where are we going?"

"To the Plaza."

---

[223] I'm getting old.

I was confused, but it's the 15th, I thought.

We left in a hurry. The whole town was empty. There were only a few cars on the street. It was weirdly quiet. Then I heard a faint noise that kept growing louder and louder. We parked and started going towards this sound. When I turned the corner, I saw hundreds of people standing. They were so loud I saw some carnival rides off to the side. There were some people in serapes. I began to smell something sweet in the air. I looked over and saw a man selling churros. It made my mouth water. There were so many people here, all of them cheering and excited.

Then I heard some bells ringing. It seemed like it was about to start. Everybody in the crowd instantly became silent. A loud voice spoke up, I couldn't see who this man was, but he kept saying name after name. Then everybody kept yelling, "Viva!"

My mom kept pulling me towards the middle, where I ran into some cousins. They just pointed to where the rest of our family was.

I heard the voice once again. "¡Viva Miguel Hidalgo!"

"¡Viva!" said everybody around me.

My mom looked at me and, with her eyes, told me to join in.

"¡Viva México!"

"¡Viva!" I whispered.

"¡Viva la Virgen de Guadalupe!" I heard.

"¡Viva!" I yelled as loud as I could.

Then there was a flood of clapping, whistling, and cheering.

It was getting quiet, then I heard panicked screaming. Followed by loud pops and bangs. I feared for the worst.

Gunshots, I thought to myself.

Then I saw a wooden structure.

"Se está quemando,"[224] I told my mom.

"No, es el castillo."[225]

---

[224] It's burning.
[225] It's supposed to, it's the castle.

"¿El castillo?"[226], I asked, confused.

Then I saw that's where the sounds were coming from. It was just shooting fireworks in all directions.

"That doesn't look safe," I said.

My mom just looked at me and told me to watch out for the torito.

"¿El torito?"[227], I asked.

Then I saw this figure rushing down the street. It was like the castillo. Only this one was on the actual street. I saw my mom get up and start running, I looked at her, and before I could run toward her, the crowd pushed in a different direction.

"Just run!" she yelled.

I looked back and saw this bull chasing after me, shooting fireworks in every direction. The adrenaline took over, and I stopped thinking. I just ran. I felt like I was running in the middle of a stampede. I had not signed up for this.

After a few seconds of seeing my life flash before me, it ran out of fireworks and stopped. Everything went back to normalcy. The air smelled like burnt gunpowder. I realized that my shirt was wet. While I tried to figure out what it was, I got a whiff of smoke and beer that had been dropped on me. It was not a pleasant combination.

I ran towards my mom, who was walking back with a bag of churros, and she asked me if I had fun.

I thought about it, *Even though there were moments where I feared for my life and felt like I was abandoned by my mother, yes, it was fun.*

Plus, she gave me a churro, so how could I not be thrilled.

The following morning, I woke up and saw my aunts in the kitchen. They had been making food since early in the morning.

---

[226] The castle?

[227] Little bull made of wood and paper mâché filled with fireworks.

There was pozole, mole, tamales, sopes, tostadas, chile rellenos, flautas, and even nopales.

It was like a full buffet. My mom told me to get ready because we had to see the rest of the city.

Everywhere we went, there were red, green, and white flowers. There were flags everywhere. People were already lining up to buy beer.

"What are we doing today?" I asked.

"Celebrar," she said.

I felt lied to. This was not like the 4th of July. It was more than just sitting down and watching fireworks in the sky. This was more intense than that. This seemed like a two-day affair as well.

We went back home to eat. And after a couple of hours of socializing and sitting around, we got ready.

My mom asked me for the newspaper.

"¿El peliodico?"

My mom looked at me and corrected me, "Pe-rió-di-co."

She was disappointed with my Spanish-speaking abilities.

"Lo estás perdiendo, y lo estas empezando hablar mocho."[228]

"How do you say electrocuted in Spanish?" She asked me.

I paused for a moment, I knew that I knew the word, but I couldn't think of it.

"Ele... ele... elecutrado... elucutrado... eleco..." I repeated to myself.

"Electrocutado," she corrected, "You're forgetting your Spanish. You need to practice more."

I was upset over the fact that she was right. I was losing my Spanish.

We finished getting ready and headed back to the plaza. I saw a man holding up a pole with the Mexican flag over his shoulders as a group of people with a green uniform followed him, marching on beat.

---

[228] You're losing it, and you're speaking it incorrectly.

After that, we heard some Mariachis playing music. They were wearing outfits that had shiny buttons. The music made me want to start moving. I looked over and saw a row of different mariachis with their big round hats and boots. That made me think of Frijolito briefly. Then I was distracted by a row of people that came onto the stage. I asked my mom who they were.

"Folclórico dancers," she answered.

The women had huge dresses. They had every color I could think of and danced beautifully. I had never seen something like that before. They all had bright polished dresses.

It reminded me of the Scarlet Macaw and about Ayden, the music made me think about Frijolito again. It was bittersweet.

The whole event turned into a party. Everybody in the street began dancing. This continued until late at night. When my body began to give out, I walked to my grandma's house, who was already in bed. I heard her coughing. I gave her a kiss goodnight and went to bed.

The next morning my mom woke me up early. It was time to go back home. I was exhausted. But it was worth it. I was so excited to tell Ayden all about it. After an hour of just saying goodbye to everybody, we were back on the road.

El Día de los Muertos

We were back a month later. I had never celebrated El Día de Los Muertos[229] before. I didn't know what to expect. I realized that the reality was far from what I had expected. It was morbid, and it didn't feel like a celebration. There weren't any mariachis playing music in full attire like I had seen on television, no colorful sugar skulls, and no food offerings. We simply lit candles and placed flowers on the graves of those we had lost.

It was the first of November, and we walked around the cemetery trying to find the graves of children who had died at a young age. We searched for my uncles' tombs. One of my uncles would have been slightly older than me. Sadly, they both died due to complications when they were born.

We were supposed to have pictures of them, but there weren't any. No pictures of them growing up and no pictures of their first days of school. They never got a chance to live. Then I realized we only had a few pictures of my grandparents. We didn't have any of my great-grandparents either. In a downhearted way, I would never know what they looked like, and there was no way to remember their faces.

We found their graves. Juan Leobardo Barrera Figueroa would have been my mom's older brother. He died moments after being born due to a lack of oxygen. Then there was Jose Alberto Barrera Figueroa. Next to him, he would have been 14 years old. I wonder what he would have been like. All we knew was that he had complications.

Both graves were small and dirty. They both had small baby shoes they never got to wear and toy cars on top of them.

---

[229] Annual Mexican celebration that honors deceased family. Day of the dead

"So, they can play with them," said my mom comforting me.

We cleaned the graves out. Brushing off any dirt that had collected. We pulled out the weeds that had been growing around and replaced all the old flowers that had been there since their birthdays. We didn't get to know them, but they were still family.

We had lunch there. It was a very depressing picnic. We all ate in silence. We didn't talk or share any stories about them. We didn't have any. The only sounds came from the wind blowing.

As we left, my mom reminded me we would return the next day. I realized that El Día de los Muertos was a two-day affair.

The following morning on November 2nd, we went back to the cemetery. There were still no food offerings or sugar skulls.

The cemetery wasn't empty like it was the day before. I could hear some music, but it wasn't happy or cheerful. It was just a few people playing guitars next to different graves. The music wasn't happy or made you want to dance. Its purpose was to remind you of what you missed.

A lonely lady roamed the cemetery, offering to sing songs to the dead. She had a beautiful red dress and walked around with a guitar. Her face was painted and only showed her skeletal remains. It was prettier than the death I was accustomed to.

We went to my grandma's grave. The cement on top of it had barely stopped drying. The gravestone wasn't even finished. All there was just a wooden cross that read, "Maria de Jesus Barrera Figueroa," my grandma's full name. The pain was still there. I saw my grandpa, and I felt sorry for him. My uncles, aunts, and cousins were all there. My uncles were sitting in the back, drinking their beers, distant from the grave. The women did most of the praying. While the children just sat there in silence, listening.

My grandma had only been buried there for a couple of days. It was difficult not to cry, but as I felt the tears coming down my cheek, I realized that El Día de Los Muertos wasn't a big deal until somebody close to the family died.

De Luto

My grandma passed away a couple of days before El Día de Los Muertos. It was a difficult realization for me. I didn't know what to make of it. She had cancer.

That day I got called into the office during class. The school had received a call from my mom. I could hear it in her voice that something was wrong.

"Tu nana se enfermo,"[230] she said bluntly, and that was it. I didn't know how to respond or what to say after that. It felt bad, and I had so many emotions to process that I felt numb.

"I'm going to pick you up. You're excused from school for the whole week."

"Where is she?" I asked.

"In an ambulance", she paused, "On her way home."

"Okay, I'll wait for you."

Why would she need an ambulance to go home? I thought.

I saw Ayden coming out of the counselor's office. He could sense my sadness, my confusion, my hurt. There was no way of hiding this.

"What happened?" he asked.

"I think my grandma passed away."

He froze, and with a heartfelt voice, he said, "Lo siento mucho."[231]

I found it unusual that he had said it in Spanish and I also pondered why he didn't question what I had just said. My grandma could have been sick. Maybe she needed my mom just how I needed her when I got sick.

"I'm sorry you have to go through that," he continued.

---

[230] Your grandma is sick.
[231] I'm sorry for your loss.

I thought he would try to cheer me up or tell me everything would be okay, but he didn't. He let me feel sad. He allowed me to have a moment of pain, of grief.

I didn't want to discuss it, but then I asked him what to expect.

"Expect?"

"Yeah, like at the funeral; I've never been to one before."

He just shrugged, "I don't know. Funerals are different for everybody."

"How was your grandma's funeral?" I asked without realizing how rude and insensitive that question must have been. But it seemed like he was in a good place emotionally to open up about it.

"Well, when my grandma died, the funeral lasted 9 days. We had a whole feast. All we did was eat and mourn. We had a whole cow, a pig, and a chicken by the time it was over. There was mole, pozole, all kinds of food."

"What else did you do during those nine days?"

"Everybody wore black," we call it "Luto."

"Luto," I repeated.

"I mean, we're not very religious, so nobody really prays, nobody uses rosaries, we just sit there and reminisce."

"Was there beer? Like your uncles drinking on the side?"

"Well yeah, but that's a given. There's always beer at every event."

"Thank you," I said. This made me feel like my family was somewhat normal.

The person at the front office informed me that my mom had arrived.

"I'll be here if you need anything," he said as I left.

I wanted to hug him, but I didn't know how. I mean, I know how to hug people. I just don't know how to be vulnerable in front of him.

I got in the car. I could tell my mom had been crying. I wanted to cry, but I needed to be strong for her, so I didn't. I also wanted to ask her questions, but I just couldn't. We took off and began our drive. The drive was quiet, but my mom kept speeding like she was trying to outrun the pain. I felt like I was not at that stage yet. I was still in the phase where it felt like a weird dream I was bound to wake up from.

We tried to find anything to distract us. We mentioned the weather seven times even though it didn't change. We focused on every song the radio played. It got a little emotional when the radio wouldn't work, and all we heard was the static, but overall, we kept it together.

That all changed as soon as we arrived. When we got to my grandparent's house, there were tons of people, some of whom I recognized, but most of them I didn't. At the moment I knew.

I avoided making eye contact with everybody. I saw my grandpa. He looked sad everywhere but in his eyes. It looked like he had been fighting back the tears. None of my uncles cried, either. I lost track of my mom, who went inside. I was lost. I didn't know what to do or how to act.

I felt pain inside of me, deep pain. I was hurt, alone, and miserable.

I didn't see any signs of food. No cows, pigs, or chickens, just stale coffee.

My aunt approached me and gave me a hug. Nobody had said anything to me. Then she told me that my grandma's body was inside and that I should pay my respects. I was too afraid to go inside but knew I had to. I couldn't avoid this any longer.

I made my way inside. I wasn't comfortable being in there. I looked over and saw my grandpa sipping on the tequila he used during special events like when my mom first returned home. It seemed like this was an appropriate time to finish the bottle.

I didn't want to be here, especially not like this. I had been in this living room many times before, but it all looked different. I saw my mom crying. I could hear her. She was loud. It was a cry full of sorrow and agony. I felt terrible for her, but I didn't feel the same pain. I was sad, but I was not suffering.

Noriega

I saw the wooden casket and noticed a glass opening where her face was. The worst part of this was that I didn't recognize the face. It resembled my grandma, but it wasn't who I remembered. I was afraid I was already forgetting what she looked like. I tried to remember her laugh or the sound of her voice, but I just felt everything slowly fading from my memory.

That's when it all became real. There was no denying that my grandma had died. I was trying hard not to cry but couldn't hold it in anymore. I felt the tears racing down my face. One of my uncles grabbed my shoulder and told me not to cry. I didn't know how else to express my emotions, but he just told me to be brave. I didn't want to be brave, but I listened.

I went outside with the rest of my uncles. None of them had cried. They had just been out there drinking. I could tell they had been drinking for a while. But once they were drunk, that's when the tears began. It was like a domino effect. I guess it was finally acceptable to be vulnerable.

I wanted to know more about my grandma's death. All I knew was that she was sick. That's all they told me, but if I was old enough to hide my emotions like a man, I was old enough to know how she died.

"¿De qué se murió?"[232] I asked while they were all crying quietly.

"Cáncer," said one of them.

"Cáncer de los pulmones,"[233] repeated another one.

Lung cancer, I thought to myself, that made me mad.

I kept asking questions, even though it was painful and made me angrier.

Turned out my grandma had tuberculosis that she had never treated properly. After years of neglect, it eventually turned into cancer. She had surgery a couple of months ago

---

[232] What did she die of?
[233] Lung cancer.

and was supposed to have died on the operating table, but she didn't.

Unluckily for her, cancer is unforgiving, and it returned a couple of months later. My grandma knew she was going to die. She felt it in her soul and decided to give up. However, she didn't want to die in the hospital. She wanted to spend her last moments in the house she spent most of her life in. The house she lived in when she got married, where she saw all her children and her children's children grow up. A house filled with love and unforgettable memories. She didn't make it there either.

When my mom heard about my grandma's condition she had not died yet. My grandma died in the ambulance on her way home. My mom wanted to get here to say goodbye to her but didn't get the chance to. That's why she sped the whole way here.

That's what hurt me the most.

"Listo pa la quinceañera," I heard one of my cousins say to me. I was glad he changed the subject.

That made a couple of my uncles laugh. They began wiping down the tears. I thought they were going to start making fun of me.

They didn't. Instead, they shared stories about my grandma's childhood. About how when she was younger, she hid in a chest when the military came to her ranch because she feared they would take her.

She was only six years old at the time. Eventually, the military left, but my grandma was so scared she stayed there for two days. I could not picture my grandma as a child. She had always been a grandma from what I remember.

Then one of my uncles pointed out that everybody that came to the funeral was from my grandpa's side. Nobody present was related to my grandma. I mean besides her children, grandchildren, and great-grandchildren.

"¿Por qué?"[234] I asked, expecting a forbidden love story, but it turned out that her mom died during childbirth when my grandma was born. They didn't have access to a hospital, and her dad, my great grandfather had been out working in the fields all day. When he came home at the end of the day, he found his daughter, but lost his wife. My grandma was completely covered in dirt, and nobody knew how long she had been lying there. Her father was in so much pain that he fell into a deep depression, and people around his community quickly realized that he was not capable of taking care of a newborn child. Somebody in the community offered to adopt her. He agreed and gave her away.

She was given to a woman that couldn't have children. So, she grew up with a family that wasn't even hers. Everybody in the community knew, so it was no secret to her. She was extremely grateful for them and always saw them as family.

That's also why we didn't know the exact date of her birthday. It's either May 3ʳᵈor 4ᵗʰ.

After she was adopted, her father moved away and started a new life. He didn't tell anybody what day she was born, and my grandma never met him.

Just like me, I thought to myself.

It was a sad way to be born, but I knew that at least I would always have one thing in common with her, which made all the pain I felt more tolerable.

Then one of my uncles told a story about how he was a "vago"[235]. So my grandma threatened to put a dress on him if he didn't get his act together. He didn't listen to her, so she got all his clothes and out of them she made him a dress.

When I asked him if he wore the dress, he just responded.

"No podía caminar desnudo"[236]

---

[234] Why
[235] Always being outside your home
[236] I couldn't walk around naked

I heard so many stories about her. I learned so many anecdotes about her life and it made me sad that I didn't know about them earlier.

I don't remember much after that. I just have memories of my uncles and grandpa holding the casket in the cemetery.

I remember that there were so many tombs and crosses of others that had lived and died before her scattered throughout the cemetery.

I remember I looked at my mom as she said her final goodbye.

I remember wanting to say goodbye, but I still had questions like, "Who would pray for me now?"

And I remember that I never did say goodbye, and I always regretted that.

Stuck at the Border

The drive back home was just as depressing as getting there. I wanted to be there for my mom but didn't know what to do. That's when I understood why she was so adamant about me going to the counselor.

I wasn't hungry when we got to the border, but I wanted to eat. Once I finished eating, I realized it wasn't what I needed. I just wanted something to distract me. I watched the train pass by. I was looking at all the graffiti on the sides. There was something peaceful about them. It was like going to an art museum and watching the art in front of you instead of having to chase paintings throughout the building.

Then the train ran out of trailers and was completely gone. I no longer had anything to entertain myself with.

"Why didn't she get medicine for cancer?" I said out loud. It was supposed to be a personal thought.

My mom didn't know what to say, "There is no cure for cancer, and she didn't have the resources to fight it."

"Do you think if she got help in the United States, she would have survived?"

She just shrugged, "No sé."

I began resenting Mexico and being Mexican, Mexicans didn't have adequate health care.

I could sense myself getting mad again. We saw one of those newspaper vendors, and I asked my mom if she had any spare change to buy me one. I wanted to get distracted from everything that was happening. After exchanging a couple of coins, I began reading.

"Hombre del Santuario Monarca Desaparecido,"[237] it said on the front page.

---

[237] Homero Gómez González missing.

The second page mentioned how there were some criminals on the run. The more I read, the more I learned about corrupt officials and drug cartels working together. I began to feel ashamed. I hated being Mexican. They didn't have anything, no good medicine, no good officials, nothing but drugs and violence.

"It's better to be American," I said to myself.

Then I turned the page. A completely different article talked about children being kept in cages. Separated at the border from their parents because they were seen as criminals. Some children's parents had already been deported, so the children were detained without knowing what would happen next because the United States couldn't locate their parents. Being American didn't sound that great, either.

Why was the United States taking away these children from their parents? And why was it a crime to want a better future?

I flipped the page and there was a different story about a teenager who died under I.C.E. custody. He was only 16 years old. It didn't say his name, but it only mentioned that he was a soccer fan and loved playing instruments.[238] It brought back unpleasant memories, so I closed the newspaper.

I couldn't control my thoughts, and curiosity began to get the best of me. Once again I felt that internal pain. I wanted my imagination to stop, but my mind continued. Maybe that was Frijolito whispered a side of my brain.

I started crying as I threw the newspaper away.

"What's wrong?" asked my mom, who was freaking out.

"Nothing, I'm fine," I snapped as I closed my eyes.

I wanted to fall asleep, and that's when I realized I hated being Mexican, but I resented being American.

Not seeing anything, but hearing the vendors, car horns and traffic. I realized I was stuck in the border of being

---

[238] Carlos Gregorio Hernandez Vasquez

Noriega

Mexican and American. I was in the middle of two worlds, but it was not a place I wanted to be in.

The Christmas Lights

The rest of the school year was not what I had expected. I guess I was still going through my emotions. Even though I knew counseling would be good for me, I stopped going. I just wanted to figure things out on my own.

I still hung out with Ayden. He stopped asking me about my family and about therapy. It was like he understood what I wanted.

After missing so much school and with projects and exams coming up, I had a lot of catching up. That's all I focused on.

I skipped soccer tryouts, and my grades were fine, but I just dug myself deeper. I became obsessed with figuring out whether it was better to be American or Mexican. They both sucked at this point. I wish I wasn't either.

And just like that the semester was over. In a blink of an eye, it was Christmas break again. My mom and I discussed going to Mexico and agreed to only go for Christmas.

The drive there was still sad but not as depressing as before, but everything had changed.

I wanted to ask my grandpa how he was doing, but it looked like he was clinging to life. He seemed unmotivated to keep living. He was alive without a purpose. He had to have some of my aunts come and take care of him. He wasn't doing well. He spoke about death like he knew it was near.

On Christmas Eve, we got ready. But it didn't feel like a celebration. We went to the cemetery and visited my grandma's grave. We cleaned it up, and I saw they had put a tombstone.

We put fresh new flowers, and then we left. It was Christmas, after all. Honestly, the food didn't taste as great as it had. That's when I realized that it had been my grandma, who was in charge of the cooking. Now it was up to my mom and aunts. My mom just kept saying, "Le falta sal,"[239] to everything, which was true. But overall, the food wasn't terrible.

That Christmas, my grandpa went to sleep early.

When midnight came, it was sad, sadder than I had expected it to be. They played the same music, and we heard the same fireworks and gunshots, but it was all different. It was our first Christmas without my grandma. At midnight nobody cheered, instead we all cried.

My mom cried, my aunts cried, my cousins cried. Even my drunk uncles cried.

I realized how normal it was seeing all my uncles drinking and my older cousins following in their footsteps. They drank at every event, birthday parties, religious holidays, regular holidays, Christmas, Easter, funerals, and basically every weekend. Like this was their way to celebrate. But what are we celebrating?

I guess that's how deep alcoholism is engraved in my family. It was so typical that nobody around me saw it as a problem, and that made me feel hopeless.

I could see my mom was worried about my grandpa, so she announced that he would be joining us for a couple of weeks. That way, he could get a change of scenery. Since he no longer worked, being alone had started to cause him to fall into a deeper depression.

I decided that it was time for me to go to sleep. I didn't have a reason to stay up. The festivities were over before they had really begun.

While trying to sleep, I heard my aunts and uncles arguing. I couldn't hear them clearly, but they talked about my mom.

They had been drinking all day, and the alcohol had gotten to them.

---

[239] Needs more salt.

One of them mentioned how my mom was only helping my grandpa because she wanted his "Terreno".[240]

My grandpa was still alive and breathing, and they were already trying to divide his land.

I was angry, but it was a type of anger that made me want to get away from here. I wanted to go back home. In a twisted way, I hoped my mom hadn't heard any of this, but a part of me wished she had.

The next morning on the 25th, we helped my grandpa pack a suitcase. My mom had already completed the paperwork and ensured my grandpa got his visa.

He had never been to the United States. He was denied a visa when he was younger and never tried to apply again.

After a couple of hours of finishing some errands and saying bye to everybody, we left. The line to cross wasn't long, so it took us a little under an hour to cross, but since it was winter, it got dark quickly, and before I knew it, the sun was gone. The moment we crossed, I saw my grandpa's eyes light up. He had never seen so many lit buildings or even street lights.

We got home at a reasonable time, but instead of going straight home, my mom took us to a neighborhood where all the houses had Christmas lights.

My grandpa's face lit up when he saw all those lights. He was acting like a little kid that had never seen lights before. Which was exactly what he was. It was heart-warming and heart-breaking. I couldn't imagine being that old and never experiencing something as simple as this.

---

[240] Land

Los Niños Héroes

I spent most of my winter break hanging out with my grandpa. I lost my room since I had to give it to my grandpa, but I didn't mind sleeping on the couch. I did mind him waking up early. I didn't know how long he was staying. Nobody did.

The weekend before school started, we decided to add an extra twin-size bed to my room. I had always been an only child and never had to share my room besides sleepovers. I was somewhat used to it, only I was sharing it with an old man, but he acted like a child. My mom had a strict no-food-in-the-room rule, but he would always sneak snacks and coffee. There would be crumbs everywhere. I would never tell, but my mom always knew.

I was worried that he would get lonely once I started going to school, and he would stay here by himself. Instead, he started picking up aluminum cans around the neighborhood. He would get up every morning and collect them for several hours. He would fill up a whole bin of them, then he would just take them to a recycling center. It didn't pay much, but it did keep him busy.

He even made friends with other old people around the neighborhood. It was like a gang of grandpas. Some of them were in wheelchairs, and others had no teeth, but they would hang out by the park and play Dominos for hours.

I noticed that he was happier, well he smiled more, that's for sure, and he drank less. He would still have a beer here and there, especially after a hard day's work, but I saw it as progress.

As for me, I avoided the counselor and distanced myself from Ayden. That didn't stop him from sitting next to me during English, Lunch, and Art. I wouldn't be rude, but I wasn't interested in discussing anything.

I still fell into moments of gray sadness, but I told myself this was normal. That it was just a part of growing up. I stopped fighting it as much and found myself okay with losing my motivation and interests.

This alarmed my mother when she saw my grades were slipping, and we had barely started the semester, but this also concerned Ayden.

One day during art, after Ayden had had enough, and confronted me.

"Xavier, I know you're sad and depressed, but I just want to let you know I'm here for you."

"I'm okay," I told him.

"No, you're not, and stop lying to yourself because the lies you tell yourself are the ones you believe the most."

"I mean, it is what it is. What can I do?"

"You fight it, you overcome your emotions, you help yourself. People don't overcome trauma by luck. It takes effort and hard work."

"I don't think I have it in me."

"You're a warrior."

I hated Ayden. Part of me just wanted to stay here. It was just easier. The other part was grateful for him; he was still struggling with so much, yet here he was, trying to get me back to my normal self.

I thanked him as I walked to my next class.

History, with Mr. Williams. I didn't have a relationship with Mr. Williams. He always wore the same 7 shirts in order. I guess he wasn't trying to impress anybody. It helped his wardrobe stay organized. This was a stark contrast to his grading and paperwork skills.

At the beginning of the school year, we were talking about cavemen. Then we talked about Native Americans for a while. However, we focused more on the conquistadors and explorers. We learned about 300 years of history in just a couple of months. Then we learned about how the United States of America was born.

This history stuff was pretty boring, plus I was on the fence between if I wanted to be Mexican or American, and seeing that the United States was older, I started leaning towards them.

One day I walked into class and sat down in my assigned seat. He continued going on about how we would go over a new period in American history.

American, I thought, daydreaming outside the window. It sounded so majestic.

Then I looked up to the board, and written in crocked, sloppy handwriting, it read, "Mexican-American War."

"We fought the Mexicans," I blurted out loud. Then I remembered what Ayden had mentioned before.

"No, we annihilated them," he repeated.

I sat up in class. It was official. I was an American. I couldn't be cheering for the losing side.

As the days went on, I learned more about this war. Mr. Williams was right. Mexico lost almost every major battle. The United States even went south and captured their castle in Mexico City.

The lesson lasted only a week. Everything that Ayden had told me was wrong. Mexico was forced to sign the "Treaty of Guadalupe Hidalgo" because they lost the war.

Why the United States didn't just take control of more territory. They could have taken all of Mexico if they wanted.

The following week I saw Ayden, and I was excited to educate him on what I had learned.

When I was his I ignored formalities.

I gave him my notebook that had all my notes. It included the quick facts about how Mexico was destroyed and how Mexico lost so much land but could have lost even more.

I saw it in his eyes. He wasn't embarrassed or ashamed about any of this. He just nodded and agreed with everything I said.

I asked him, "How can you be proud of that?"

"Well, what gives you pride, to begin with?" he asked rhetorically.

"Mexican culture and history gives me pride," he continued, "There's so much that Mexico represents to me that cannot be taken away. See, that's what this country does. The United States takes everything away from you. Your sense of identity and individuality don't exist here. People are stripped from their identity because so much history is erased here."

I stood there in silence. I don't know what I was expecting would happen. Of course, he would know more than me.

"You know how you said that the United States military went to Mexico City and overtook "El Castillo de Chapultepec?" Well, we don't see that as an embarrassment. We take great pride in what happened there. That hill was a symbolic place for the Aztecs. Then it became the house of European emperors who governed us. It was even a military academy and is currently a museum. There's a lot of history there."

"You said you didn't see that final battle as an embarrassment. Why not? Mexico lost the war," I asked.

"We did, but have you heard of Los Niños Heroes?"

He looked at me like he expected me to know who they were. Like always, I just looked back until he started talking.

"During the battle, the castle didn't have enough soldiers, so General Bravo ordered them to retreat because they were heavily outnumbered, but 6 children refused and stayed back"

"Children?"

"Yeah, they were in military school and were from 13 to 19 years old."

I paused and reflected.

"Well, all 6 of them were from different regions of Mexico, so they basically represented all of Mexico. They all stayed behind to guard the entire castle against the United States army. They fought for as long as they could, except for Juan Escutia. He didn't want the Mexican flag to be under the United States' possession, so he wrapped himself in the flag and jumped off the castle. He died on impact. Juan had enlisted in the academy a couple of days earlier, but what he lacked in experience, he made up for with valor. I mean, all of them were heroic, Juan de la Barrera, Francisco Márquez, Agustín Melgar, Fernando Montes de Oca, Vicente Suárez, and Juan Escutia were all so young, but they showed so much courage and bravery that day."

I just reflected on what he had said.

Juan de la Barrera, I thought to myself. *Just like me.*

Xavier Barrera

"You know, not every American soldier was proud of what they did during that war. You should look up St. Patrick's Battalion."

I nodded my head, and I wrote it down so I wouldn't forget.

When I got home, my mom was in her room, and my grandpa was already asleep. I heard the phone ring but didn't pick it up on time. I went to my mom's room. I opened her door cautiously. She was just sitting in her bed. The television was off, there was no book in her hands or music on. Her lights were all off.

I let myself in, "Buenas noches, ama"

She just sat there. For a second, I didn't know if she was asleep.

Then I felt her move, "Hey, Xavier."

She moved and started facing me directly, and I asked her what she knew about St. Patrick's battalion.

She just stared at me blankly. Like I was making this up. I asked her to take me to the library, or anywhere I could learn more about them.

She refused, "No," she said.

Why did she say no.

It was quiet, and she continued talking.

"How's school going?"

I was not interested in talking about school right now.

Then she asked me, "Have you gone to the therapist."
I lied and told her I had tried to schedule an appointment.
"Have you actually tried?"
I didn't want this lie to get bigger, so I told her the truth.
"Mom, I don't want to go anymore."
I was expecting a long lecture, even some sort of discussion, but she didn't say anything.
All I got was a disappointed look. I didn't know what to make of it.

A History of Trauma

I woke up early the next morning. The sun was barely peeking out as I went to the school library. All I took was a notebook, and I just dove into my research.

I researched what I could about St. Patrick's Battalion. I was fascinated with what I was learning, but this wasn't enough.

I decided that I had to go back to the beginning. There was probably so much I was missing out.

I searched for information about the Aztecs. I wanted to know more about their folktales, who their emperors were, and ultimately what caused their demise. I wanted to know anything I could about their culture. I studied their myths and legends. I even stumbled across Mexican Medusa, Coatlicue, she didn't turn people into stone, but she was the snake lady in charge of creation and destruction. I was just captivated by their way of life. I dedicated all my free time to this. It became an obsession. I knew there was more to uncover, and I was hungry to see what else was out there.

After a couple of weeks, I learned that Mexico became a country on September 27th, 1821, but they declared independence from Spain on September 16th, 1810.

I learned about political figures like Agustín I of México, Guadalupe Victoria, Benito Juarez, Francisco Villa, and Emiliano Zapata.

I dove into art and discovered who Frida Kahlo was. I learned she was born the same year a Mexican railroad brakeman named Jesús García Corona gave his life to save the city of Nacozari by leading a train filled with dynamite away from the city.

I followed history chronologically, I read about "La Matanza" in the 1930s, where they lynched Mexicans in

Texas, and about the mass deportation efforts of Mexican American citizens called the "Mexican Repatriation."

Every day I would uncover more and more history. Slowly building my own identity.

I learned about the Zoot Suits and how actors like "Tin-Tan" and activist Cesar Chavez wore them. But sadly, they were associated with gang attire and seen as unpatriotic, ultimately leading to the "Zoot Suit Riot." Where Mexican Americans were beaten and killed in the streets of Los Angeles. I wondered why so much of this information had been kept from me.

Then I realized that there were two Cesar Chavezes, only one of them was named Julio Cesar Chavez. Then there was another figure called Oscar De La Hoya. There were so many people I wanted to research.

I didn't know what thread to follow, in music there was Ritchie Valens and Pedro J. Gonzalez, in television there was Rosanna DeSoto and Dolores del Río. In politics there was Don Pío Pico along with Roy Benavidez and Padre Kino.

There was so much to discover, but that didn't stop me from seeing what else I could find. I learned that in 1946, the Mendez family in California fought because they believed segregated schools were unconstitutional.

I wrote until I filled up the final page, and I closed my notebook. I felt accomplished and like I finally had enough to share with Ayden.

The next day I waited for Ayden. I wanted to let him know everything I had found out. I wanted to share everything I was proud of and everything that I was disappointed in.

I saw Ayden coming out of the counselor's office. I had not seen him come out of there in a while.

"How you been?" I asked him.

"Better," he said and asked, "How's your project coming along?"

I looked at him and showed him the notebook.

"This is impressive," he said to me.

Noriega

"Yeah, I just started researching the "Dirty Mexican War"" I said.

"Yes, that is an unfortunate part of our history," he paused, "The United States doesn't like other countries to progress. Sometimes I even think they don't want to progress either."

"What do you mean?"

"I mean, you researched history and learned about social injustices and important figures. That's something history frequently teaches us about. I mean, look at this country. Why do you think people migrate here? Is it because there are more resources here? Do you think that people here are smarter? What do they have here that makes this country so great? Do you think that English is a superior language? What makes the United States different is that they have perfected history by sugarcoating all the injustices they have committed and never admitting their mistakes."

I didn't know what to say after that. I could sense that his tone had changed. He seemed distant. Maybe he was upset with me for ignoring him the last couple of months.

He looked at me, "I mean, this is all great, but what's the point of history if you don't learn from it? You need help. I think you are trying to escape your emotions by covering up your feelings. I mean, I get it. Don't get me wrong, I see that you are proud about being Mexican, as you should be, but you're more than just Mexican. But where you're from shouldn't and doesn't define you. You're human at the core of everything and need to help yourself."

I knew that he was right.

He looked over my notebook as he flipped through the pages.

"Go to therapy, and then we can talk about this, there's a lot of pain in our history, but there's also healing. Remember, you can't find who you are if you don't help yourself first."

I knew he was right, right about history and right about what I was going through. And he was right about what I needed. I needed help, and I was finally going to get it.

La Mariposa

I decided that I had to go back to counseling. Somewhere deep inside me, I knew it was for the best. In the back of my head, I knew what Ayden had said was right. I hated to admit that, but I knew facing my problems was better.
When I got home, I decided to confess to my mom what I was feeling.
"I'm not okay, and I know that. I've decided to go to therapy and get help."
She gave out a sigh of relief, and I saw tears going down her face. I didn't understand why she had gotten so emotional. I looked at her and asked her not to tell my grandpa.
"Okay, mijito," she said as she hugged me tightly.
The next morning. I woke up early like I had been, but instead of going to the library, I went to the counselor's office.
I didn't know how to act or what to feel. I was excited, nervous, but also embarrassed.
I arrived before Ms. Jimenez, and when she got there, she greeted me.
"Buenos Dias."
Damn, everybody here knows Spanish. Even people who don't seem like they would.
I didn't know what I was expecting, I was afraid that she would be sarcastic or mock me for coming back, but she didn't do any of that.
Instead, she asked me, "Would you like to come in?"
It was like I had the power. I could decide if I wanted to come inside or if I didn't. We both knew I was there because I wanted help.
I sat down, and she asked me, "What brings you here?"

"I guess I recently realized that I need help. That I'm not okay, and I'm actually hurting."

I felt the tears coming down. There was so much to unpack, but this was in a safe place, free of judgment and expectations. A place where I could be who I was and show what I felt.

I opened up about my grandma and confessed how much I missed her. The fact that I couldn't let my emotions out had led me to keep them bottled in. I think that it was normal to mourn over somebody that had died. Especially since I knew so little about her. I never got to fully understand what I meant to her. I didn't get to say goodbye or tell her how much I loved her. I wish she knew how much I missed her. I just had so much regret.

I wanted to recall every memory I had about her. Her voice, her laugh. I wanted to keep every memory I had of her.

It felt good to open up, and just like that, my tears had washed away. I felt lighter, emotionally.

Then I heard the morning bell, she wrote me a pass in case I was late and told me that she would see me the following week. Same time.

I wanted to thank her, but instead, I asked, "Why didn't you force me to come?"

She looked at me and replied "Only you can decide when you're ready to stop struggling and ready to start healing."

During class, I could not stop thinking about everything that happened.

I saw Andrea walk in and felt like I had not seen her in years. I waved at her. I could not believe that somebody so pretty was related to somebody so dorky. Then her brother walked in.

I was so excited to see him like I wanted to tackle him and thank him on the ground, but I tried to be cool about it.

I just nodded at him, and he looked at me, "How was therapy?"

"Oh, you know," I said smiling as I wiped tears off my face.

"That makes me happy," he said with a sense of relief.

We took our seats then Ms. Maynard began talking about our end-of-the-school-year essay. It was our final project and would make up a large portion of our grade. I could not believe that the school year was already almost over.

"This essay will mirror the essay you wrote at the beginning of the school year. The only difference is that this essay is going to be a self-reflection. I want you to realize how much you grew and how much of your identity was formed in this past year alone," she said.

I had no clue what I was going to write about.

I looked over at Ayden, and I could see him writing notes down. He was filled with ideas. As for me, I was clueless.

"Want to come over so we can work on this?" I asked.

"Sure," he said.

"Only I take the bus home. I don't have a fancy professional driver like you," I laughed.

"My parents drive recklessly. They wouldn't make it as professional drivers," he stated in a matter-of-fact tone.

I just laughed. Everything he said was so serious.

During that lunch, we just talked. We had many conversations, catching up on the last couple of months.

Then we walked to art class. We had been working on this project for weeks, and Ayden was almost finished with his work. While all I had were a couple of random lines and no inspiration. I had a feeling I would fail this class, but I had a couple of weeks to pull this off.

After school, Ayden's mom offered us a ride to my house instead of having to take the bus. When we got home, my mom and my grandpa were already there. They were both at the kitchen table. My grandpa was sharing what had happened during dominoes that day, which was pretty much the same thing that usually happened to him daily.

My mom recognized Ayden and just winked at me. It was kind of embarrassing. I was too old for my mom to be proud of me for having a friend.

After that, we went to my room, and we sat on different beds, took out our notebooks, and had everything out like we were going to start doing homework and studying.

"Why do you have two bed?" he asked.

"I share my room with my grandpa."

"Since when?" he asked.

I just looked at him, "Look Ayden, I'm sorry I've been distant, a lot has changed for me over the last few months. My mom brought him to stay for us for a while, she thought a change of scenery would be good for him, and it seemed to have helped."

"Thank you for sharing", he responded.

I was annoyed, but I was curious about his art project, so since he had asked me personal questions I began to ask him about his drawing. He had been enigmatic about it.

"You can only see my work once it is finished," he said.

I hated waiting and had secretly looked at his sketches, but only saw drafts of his final piece.

"Why are you drawing a snake?" I confronted him.

He looked at me, somewhat annoyed. Like he knew that I knew.

"I'm not. That was just an idea."

"What's with the snake obsession?"

"It's not an obsession. Snakes have always been a symbol to the Aztecs for wisdom, birth, and creation."

"Why?" I asked him.

"If you think about it, no animal is closer to the earth than the snake."

"That explains Coatlicue." I said, "Then why did Mexico have an eagle eating a snake on its flag?"

"It's complicated, you see, according to an old Aztec legend, the Aztecs wandered the land trying to find a place to build their capital. Once they saw an eagle standing on top of a cactus, they knew where they would build their city."

"Nopales. It's always nopales" I said.

"But that still doesn't explain why the snake is being eaten." I added.

"That was added later by the Europeans. It was a way for them to symbolize that Christianity had ruled over the Indigenous tribes. What better way to control a population if you take the image of what they are most proud of and depict it being eaten onto their national flag?"

I could not understand why Mexicans were like this, how they could have so much pride in their country after all these injustices.

Just then, I saw a butterfly flying outside through the window.

That gave Ayden an idea.

"You can write your final English paper about the Monarch Butterfly," he said.

"You can also illustrate it for Art class," he added.

"Why?" I asked him.

"Because they are known for traveling from the United States to Mexico and they symbolize growth. It would be perfect for you."

I thought about it for a second.

"You can be la mariposa," he said.

I hated everything about that.

Llamadas Pérdidas

I felt good. I was at peace with myself.
I was no longer afraid of being who I was. I realized I
wouldn't allow society to dictate who I would be. I'm
Mexican, but I'm more than just lotería, churros, and
nopales. I know that Mexicans are Mexican all the time and
that I'm only Mexican part-time. It no longer bothered me to
think that I was different. I stopped seeing myself as an
individual but rather as my own little Mexican-American
community.

Before leaving on summer break, I stopped at Ms.
Jimenez's office.

"We still have some progress to make." she reminded
me.

"I promise we will catch up once school starts."

"Maybe I'll see you for summer school," she said.

I had completely forgotten about that.

"I have to go check on my classes and see about that," I
said.

I already knew I had passed Maths, Science, History, and
P.E. It was the other two classes that worried me.

I walked into my English class and picked up my final
essay. Seeing my final grade made me anxious; but there it
was, "C-." That meant that I wouldn't have to take summer
school for English.

Honestly, it was a lot better than what I was expecting. It
was easier to identify with an insect than I had expected.

"I loved the idea of you transforming from a caterpillar
to a butterfly, but your writing needs some work," she said.

I thanked Ms. Maynard for her help and patience. I felt
guilty since the idea that saved me wasn't even mine. Maybe
I was more American than I thought.

Then I ran to art class.

Noriega

I saw a post-it note on my unfinished canvass. Just some strokes of ink trying to stand for an unfinished butterfly.

"F," in dark red ink.

"You know this is supposed to be abstract."

I told my art teacher, "It could be worth millions in a museum someday"

"That's great, but today and in here, it's worth an F; see you in summer school," said Mr. Paulson.

I was feeling pretty bummed when I saw Ayden, "Here you go," he said as he handed me his painting. He had it framed and signed it at the bottom.

"I can't turn this in," I told him, "Mr. Paulson already knows you drew this. Plus, it has your signature."

He gave me a side-eye, "It's not for that. It's for you. I want you to have it."

"Why?"

"Because it represents who you are."

I looked at the painting. It was the emblem on the Mexican flag, except it was from a different perspective.

"You see, I used a Bald Eagle, the symbol of freedom in the United States, instead of a Golden Eagle, which is used on the Mexican flag. I used the image of cactus since they symbolize Mexico but left the snake out of it."

"So, you're saying I was your model and inspiration for this."

Ayden rolled his eyes and ignored my comment. He proceeded to change the topic.

"We're leaving tonight, so we will probably be there around the same time as you. Are you sure you don't want a ride?"

"I'm okay, I want to just take the scenic route, and maybe I'll see the Monarch Butterflies or stop at the Sanctuary."

"We're taking the same route," he responded.

There was a pause, and he continued, "And I think the sanctuary is closed," in a cheerless tone.

"Oh…" I said.

I could tell he had gotten sad, but I didn't understand why.

"Anyways," I continued, "I'll be there, I promise," I said with a smile.

"Alright," he said, smiling back.

Before leaving, I looked up at the sky and saw it was cloudy.

"I think it might rain," I said.

"Yeah, I love the smell of petrichor,"[241] he responded.

"What the hell does that mean?" I asked.

Before he could answer, I hugged him. I could tell I caught him off guard because it was the first time I asked him a question and he was speechless.

I didn't know what to do next, so I ran away.

"I'll see you tomorrow," I yelled.

As I caught the city bus to get home, I looked up at the clouds, and I didn't feel myself getting sad. If anything, I was a little excited.

It started raining lightly as soon as I got inside the house. The water barely missed me, and my mom was already rushing me because my bus was leaving soon.

She gave me Andrea's and Ayden's Quinceañera invitations.

"You won't be able to get inside the party without this," she said.

"I highly doubt that, Mom. I will be staying with them for a while."

"Oh yeah, does that mean you don't have summer school?" she asked.

"No, I do."

"How many classes did you fail?"

"One," I said, "Art class."

"Who fails art class?" She asked me.

---

[241] The smell that accompanies the first rain.

The idea of summer school haunted me. That is not how I wanted to spend my summer, but I didn't want worry about that now.

My mom was getting her bags ready, she wasn't coming with me, and we weren't going on our usual trip to Mexico. Instead, she was taking my grandpa to Vegas. I guess he wanted to see more lights like he had during Christmas.

I finally got my bags ready after being rushed by my mom. I double-checked to make sure I had everything. I was on my way out with my luggage and a folder filled with documents I needed when I heard the phone ring.

My mom told me to ignore it and that it was "Probably somebody calling about our extended warranty."

I ignored her and went to the phone.

"Apúrate,"[242] I heard my mom yelling from the car. "You're going to miss the bus, and I'm not driving you all the way there."

When I answered the phone I instantly recognized the voice on the other side, and I couldn't help but smile.

"Hola," he said, "Te he estado hablando."[243]

---

[242] Hurry up.
[243] I've been calling you.

Made in United States
Troutdale, OR
11/11/2024

24682701R00148